ISBN-13: 978-1478352938

ISBN-10: 1478352930

Cover photograph by Kourtney Selak, contact website www.wix.com/kourtneyselak/photography

For my mother, Kelly. Your strength inspires me daily.

"I got off track, I made mistakes.

Back slid my way into that place where souls get lost,

Lines get crossed,

and the pain won't go away.

I hit my knees, now here I stand!

There I was, now here I am…

Here I am,

Changed."

-Changed, Rascal Flatts

Pieces of a Mending Heart

Kristina M. Rovison

Chapter 1

Loathing clings to you like thousands of miniscule spider webs, invisible yet entirely encompassing. No amount of time, nor wind or rain can wash the webs from your soul. Buried deep within, they claw their way deeper into your flesh, until all you see, all you feel, is their spiny fingers gripping tighter with your every move. Their vice-like presence sends a fog over you, in which you comprehend nothing, feel nothing, see or hear nothing. Nothing, but the hatred that fills your heart with every step you take. Still breathing, still walking, blinking, eating and drinking; in every physical way, you are technically human.

What people can't see is the screaming madness within, slowly seeping towards the surface of a visibly healthy looking person. What people can't see is the red of your blood turning to gray nothingness as your heart beats out the contempt that floods your inner being. The body is a shell, nothing more than a fleshy exterior that is not only temporary, but breakable. It can function on autopilot for days, weeks, years, without ever having a connection to the person possessing it.

This is the beginning of what I thought was the end, the time I would end my suffering here on Earth and join the loved ones from my past. Shivering, though the water was burning hot, I sit in the bathtub, holding the knife in my right hand. "Goodbye," I think to myself. There is no point in saying the words out loud when no one is here to hear me say them. As soon as the word echoes through my brain, the notebook that contains my suicide letter drops off the counter to the floor with a thwack.

It was surprisingly easy to make my decision, the quickness of the cold blade against the vulnerable skin of my wrists. I sit in my parents' bathtub as I slash away my woes, each drop of blood hitting the water like a burden off my shoulders. Nothing happens the way I thought it would, though. No flashing bright lights, no trumpets sounding from Heaven, not even the cliché "flash-back" moments seen in countless movies. Just, nothing. Nothing but the pain in my wrists and the thumping of a long dormant heart…

It has been so long since I've felt anything; it's been forever since my heart seemed to beat in tune with my mind. I heard once, somewhere, that the mind stays living a few seconds after the body dies. Whether or not this is true, I can't be certain, especially now. It feels as if I have been lying here forever, sitting, waiting for the burdens to be swept away.

Then, I hear it. I didn't know that light was something that could be heard, but I know instantly what it is. I open my eyes and see myself, lying fully clothed in my parents' bathtub, face inches below the surface of the water. Looking down at myself, I barely recognized the skinny body that I had once called my own. The light, a ringing in my ears that is indescribable, urges me to look up from the dead body below me.

I look up to see a man standing there, not three feet away from me. If my heart was still beating, it would have been sent into overdrive.

"Katherine, what a fool you have been my child," the man says.

I do nothing, refusing to speak, but I feel my mouth open. Instead of sound, words fall out. Literally, *words* fall to the ground, rising through my throat, leaving their bitter taste on my tongue, and passing my lips as they clatter to the ground in an organized array. Not forming any specific sentences, the various words shape themselves into a square formation, their bold letters standing out from the pale tiles of the bathroom floor.

"Read them," commands the man.

Having no choice but to obey, I sink to my knees as I read the words sprawled on the floor. Aloud, I begin to read: "greed, jealousy, hatred, lust, bitterness, grief, fear, shame, blame, regret, remorse, apathy, refusal…"

The voice that says the words sounds like my own, but I am not in control of my vocal cords at the moment. My entire being feels like it is being electrocuted, hair standing on end and skin whirring with energy. I look down at my hands, flexing and bunching my muscles, feeling the smooth skin of my long fingers gliding along each other.

"Who are you?" I ask the man, feeling the need to avert my eyes from his gaze.

"Dear Katherine, you have made a rather unwise decision, have you not?" he says with a grim look on his face as he gestures to my lifeless body in the water.

Again, I feel the need to look away when speaking to him, as if his skin is emitting a bright invisible light. The ringing in my ears ceases when he speaks, as if the world around us is drowned out simply by his presence.

"Who are you?" I repeat, growing slightly panicked. Where is Heaven? If I don't deserve Heaven, where is Hell? Something, anything, would be better than having to stare at the body I have willingly chose to leave. There's something eerie about having to watch myself bobbing up and down in the steamy red water, and I'm not feeling much at peace.

"Katherine," he says, placing his hand on my shoulder. The moment he touches me, my woes disappear. Like the steam from the water that helped end my life, they float to the ceiling of the bathroom and cloud the mirror with their dreariness. "Katherine, why have you chosen to end the life I have given you? These words," he gestures towards the pile of words on the floor, "hold an opportunity. I cannot allow you to enter my Kingdom when it is not your time. My daughter, so much is in store for you. Tell me, what made you think life was so worthless? What made you think your problems weren't something we could work through together? I have plans for you, Katherine," he finishes, shaking his handsome head.

I feel the desire to drop to my knees and beg for forgiveness. What have I done? God is standing before me, telling me how disappointed he is in my decisions and I have no chance to undo my wrongs. I killed myself to leave my demons behind, but if I paid attention to the years of church sermons I had attended, I would have known my sins could not be washed away with death.

What now? There are no words for what I am feeling; there is nothing but despair and longing... longing for a second chance. There is nothing, no erratic heartbeat, no heaving for air or salty tears to stain my cheeks. For the better part of my life, this is what I wanted. I ached to be devoid of any emotions at all and be spared from a broken heart. There is too much pain, too little happiness and too much sorrow, so it would be best not to feel at all in this world I feel so disconnected from.

I was dead wrong. There is not a thing I wouldn't do to change the fact that I am unfeeling at this moment. The despair that filled me moments ago is gone, replaced by a terrifying nothingness that seems to sink into my core. This scares me more than anything ever has before, because I can *feel* myself slipping away into a black pit of bleak emptiness.

I feel the weight of a hand on my head and look up, forcing the fingers to slip away. I immediately crave their warmth, the happiness they bring with their touch, but God speaks to me and his words fill my heart with hope.

"Katherine, you know you made a mistake. You know it is too late to reverse the unchangeable. But Katherine, what you don't know is of my willingness to give you a second chance. You possess a truly magnificent soul, my child. A soul fashioned in my image; a soul that needs nothing more than love and kindness to bring it out of the depths you continually fall into.

"Stand up," God continues, grasping my cold hands in his warm ones. "These words are so much more than they appear. These words are the key to your eternal happiness. If you wish to be granted a second chance, this is your only opportunity. There is so much in you. You need to fight the darkness and not give into it!" he says passionately, making my eyes widen.

"Heaven is not ready for you, my child. And, quite frankly, you are not ready for Heaven. If you wish to be granted a second chance, say the words and your heart will start beating again. You've made this choice before, so listen to your soul."

My mouth opens, words threatening to explode into the quiet room around us. A second chance? Am I really willing to go back to the world I intentionally left? There is no time for drawn out decisions, it is now or never. Literally.

Without my consent, my voice fills the room. "Please," it says, my eyes falling closed and head bowing.

I can feel God's smile burning into my skin, filling me with a yearning I didn't know existed. "My child, you will do wonderful things. I have sent you an angel, the one to bring you from darkness and into the light. Keep your eyes open, Katherine, because he is not an angel in your sense of the word," God continues, quietly.

"What are the words for, Father?" I ask meekly.

"These," he again motions towards the square on the floor, "are what you must face when you return. They are your punishment, but also a necessity. Your soul has been fractured for too long, child. Your back has been turned and these are the reciprocations."

"Sir, if I deserve punishment, why are you giving me a second chance?" I ask, unable to ignore my curiosity.

"Katherine, punishment is different than damning you to an eternity in Hell," he says patiently. "Not one of my children is perfect, but all are worthy of a second chance. I will send you back to Earth, but you will face the consequences of your act. These words I have laid out will be experienced by you; emotions and situations that you will inevitably experience. These experiences will transform you into who you need to be. You have spent so much time cutting me out, Katherine. It is time you feel again, and this is where you begin."

He walks towards my dead body and I notice for the first time that he is barefoot. There is a halo of azure blue light around his head, which surprises me considering the person in which it surrounds. I thought halos were supposed to be yellow or orange, not blue.

Without warning, he turns around, smiling peacefully. "Blue is your favorite color, Katherine. I am everything you have ever loved and more. My Kingdom is waiting for you, but you must let *me* make the proper decisions. You must fight Satan and sin, because there will be no more chances. Look for your angel, he will make everything right again," he finishes.

"Will I experience these all the time, Father?" I whisper, feeling fearful.

God offers me a small smile. "No, Daughter, you will not. When the time comes, you will feel them much stronger than anyone else ever has, but if you follow the course you're meant to follow, your time in Earthly purgatory will be short. This is your punishment, but it will make you stronger, Katherine; this will right your wrongs. Not feeling has been an option for you for far too long. Not everything in this world is evil, despite what you may think," he shakes his head sadly.

"Father?" I say as he continues to look at me, "I am sorry I betrayed you. I am sorry I am not who I was meant to be." My eyes feel strange, as if being pricked by needles, as if I am crying tears of vinegar. I cry out, hands coming to my face, but God stops me.

"Katherine, you are exactly who you are meant to be. All your conscious mind has to do is find that strand that connects your inner-mind to your heart, and it will. Do good with the gifts you are given, child," he says, placing his hand on my head. The pain immediately subsides, leaving me breathless as I watch wisps of black smoke float to the ceiling of the steam filled bathroom.

God seems to notice my distraction and gestures to the smoke. "Your sins," is all he says.

"Thank you, Father. I will do my best," I say, looking in his eyes, which are an indescribable green-blue color. Almost like turquoise.

"Your angel will be searching for you as well, Katherine. Be happy, my child. He is your light," the Lord says, walking backwards until he stands in the water of the bath with my dead body.

Never turning his back on me, he puts both his hands out in front of him and splays his fingers in the air over my chest. The bathroom door opens with a squeak and my mother walks in, head down. As she sees my body, I hear her intake of breath before a strangled sob escapes her mouth. She screams and I feel myself slipping. The Lord's face is the last thing I see before my world flips to black.

Chapter 2

Five months later, I am sitting in the first class section of the airplane destined for Shields Valley, Montana- population 2,013. My parents have decided it is best for me to take a break from the fast paced life of a seventeen-year-old Chicago girl and to spend a bit of time breathing in the crisp Montana air.

I will spend my senior year in a new school, boarding with an aunt I have met no more than three times in my young life. It seems to get an extended vacation all one needs to do is add "mentally unstable" to their rap sheet. The irony of life and its' simplicities…

My mind flashes to the day I woke up in the hospital's psych ward. The lumpy pillow under my head, squeaky bed wrapped in cellophane, flimsy white sheet lying on top of me, and the man standing just outside my door, all added to a very dramatic wake-up. My once icy mother turned into a doting stranger as she took in the bandages wrapped around my wrists, carrying on about how sorry she was that I felt like I didn't have anyone to turn to.

She is a coward. This is not the first time one of her children has been in the nuthouse, you see. My older brother, David, committed the same heinous act that I did; it must be hereditary to feel the desire to pull your own plug. When I was fifteen, I remember feeling panic as I raced through the house to get the telephone, terrified I wouldn't get help in time. Like the cowards they were, my parents sent him away to a reform school in Toronto. He never came back.

No, he didn't die. He just got smart. David writes to me twice a month, telling me to be strong and that things will get better. But the thing is they aren't getting better. My parents, who I would be lucky to see for an hour every day, have *never* been my parents. Blood is nothing but an Earthly tie to these deplorable bodies we are forced to possess.

PANG. A knife is twisted into my stomach as I feel the hatred creep in. Like physical pain, I feel the burn twirling my intestines into a jumble of pebbles, leaving a stinging ache in its wake. I take a deep breath, focusing on the pleasant things in life.

Thankfully, the hatred subsides quickly. I am not angry with God, you see. I am angry at my parents for being who they are. Actually, I have become what many teenagers would call a "religious freak" since my "death" five months ago, but there is no possible way to explain my meeting with God to anyone without getting chucked right back into the ward, so I keep that little tidbit to me, myself and I.

I remember everything that happened that night with sharper clarity than I have remembered anything before. Meeting God is not something I have ever considered, ever actually thought about happening. Sure, I didn't think suicide was very serious at the time. I never considered whether or not I would wake up in heaven or hell, which was actually the point. I just never wanted to wake up.

The drugs weren't helping much in my decision making at the time, but now I'm cleaner than a preacher's daughter. Doing drugs was my escape; they were the only things that made me *feel*. It's pretty impressive actually, getting away with using drugs for as long as I did. The private all-girls Catholic high school wasn't as observant as they should have been and, being the rebellious teen that I was, I took full advantage of the fact.

I run my fingers over the fading scars on my left wrist, the constant reminder of not only my breaking point, but of my meeting with God. He told me to look for my angel, so I have ardently been keeping my eyes open. There was a boy on my street named Angel, but I had never spoken to him because he was three years younger than me. There was the occasional attractive stranger that caught my eye and even some fellow head-cases in the hospital, but none of them seemed any different than anyone else. I'm expecting fanfare: strobe-lights, trumpets, 'Hallelujah' and '*Hark the herald angels sing*' playing in the distance as the lights dim… you know, the whole shebang.

Since I met God- which I've grown to refer to as "the meeting" – I feel the way I felt before I grew up, at the time where complete innocence embraced me.

Feeling the anger creep back into my blood, I take a deep breath and come back to the present. My angel better show himself pretty soon, or else I might have to resort to drastic measures.

Maybe an ad on Craigslist, I joke to myself. Thinking about my angel makes me wonder… Is he going to be my age? A best friend? A lover? A teacher, maybe? Just an inspiring, influential person to bring me avoid the pit that is eternally hovering around my ankles?

Maybe I should stop looking for him. If it's destined by God that we meet, it will happen soon enough. I trust Him wholly, believing with all my heart that my elusive protector will be someone fantastic. Just thinking about the possibilities sends my heart into an uneven gallop, flushing my face and gracing my features with a small, rare smile.

I hear the mechanical whirring sounds that could only mean the plane is about to take off. As predicted, the pilots' voice filters through the speakers, thanking everyone for flying with them today. I block it all out, tracing the thick scars on my wrist and humming. The plane jolts forward, momentarily sending my stomach into a nervous knot. There is no reason to fear flying, but there's a first time for everything and I've never been on a plane before.

The aircraft rockets forward and begins to ascend, leaving the city behind and all the memories it holds. Whether this is a blessing or a curse is unknown to me, but that's the beauty of it all. I'm not running away from the past, but rather embarking on a new adventure. The future is mysterious and unknown and both adjectives fill most people with anxiety or nervousness, but not me. No, right now all I can think of is the joy of becoming a new person, full of excitement at the opportunities ahead. Right now, all I can think of is finding my angel.

* * *

A few hours later, I end up in the backseat of my Aunt Rachel's car. Not only does it smell like baby powder, *heavily*, but also like roses. Not the smells that I'm used to, but I immediately associate this with new beginnings. Hopefully, though, the rest of my adventure won't be as… girly. I'm not a tomboy, don't get me wrong, but I don't like smelling like old ladies who fell in a rosebush.

The car ride is awkward to say the least, having to sit in the backseat because my luggage took up every other available space. Silence fills the heavy air with its uncomfortable deadness, and even the static-filled radio can't relieve the tension floating through the air.

"So, Katherine, are you excited?" Aunt Rachel chimes in, taking a puff of a cigarette.

I hesitate before answering. Excited for what, exactly? Living with her? Not at all exciting. Awkward and unnatural? Yeah.

"Yes, Aunt Rachel. I'm looking forward to experiencing new things," I say, politely cool.

She snorts softly. "Well honey, I don't blame you for wanting to get away from that house," she said, bitterness lacing her tone.

She's always hated my father. At least we have one thing in common. I smirk. "Will it just be you and me at the house?" I asked quietly.

Aunt Rachel looks at me briefly in the rearview mirror before taking another puff of her cigarette. "Sure thing, honey. It's a tiny little ranch, but you'll like it a lot there, don't you worry. I have you all set to start school next week Monday and all your supplies and whatnot are waiting in your room. I hope you like blue, because I painted the walls myself. I thought I remembered you saying it was your favorite color when you were just a little tot," she trails off, giggling a bit.

I wasn't sure if I liked the endearment "honey." Sure, it was sweet sounding to others, but to me, it sounded condescending. If there is one thing I cannot stand, it's being pitied or looking down upon.

"Whatever you have for me is just fine, Aunt Rachel. Thank you," I say, still rigidly decorous.

Suddenly, the car stops. It sputters for a moment before kicking off completely. With my suitcases stacked on either side of me, I can't see out the windows. I don't know where we were until I hear, "We're home!"

The door is wretched open and my suitcase tumbles to the ground, letting the brisk air attack my sensitive skin. At first, I'm mortified by the little house in front of me. Then, before I get the chance to say something out loud, I see the vast, open sky in front of me. My eyes can't seem to adjust to the disarming brightness before me, and I'm forced to squint from the light of the setting sun. It's chilly, but the calmness of the quiet soothes my gooseflesh.

"What do you think?" Aunt Rachel asks, gesturing towards the little house a few yards away.

The house *is* tiny; Rachel was right, it's more like an apartment. Not in building structure, but in sheer size. Why would anyone waste building such a small house on such a beautiful piece of land? The green seems to stretch on for miles, which it probably does. Off in the distance, I see the faces of mountains, their tips glistening in the setting sun. It looks like a postcard, like *the* postcard Rachel sent me years ago. The only postcard I ever got from her, but I treasured it for its beautiful photograph.

Speechless, I stand there and continue to ogle at the marvelous beauty in front of me. Instantly, I fall in love with the landscape, feeling its fresh openness seep into my deprived bones. "I love it," I whisper, just loud enough for her to hear.

"You see that?" She points to a small building, probably a half a mile away. I nod. "That's the stable. There's three horses in there, if you wanna learn to ride some time. It's pretty relaxin', having all this space and nothing to do. You ever feel like going exploring, go on horseback," she finishes, taking my suitcase into the house.

Oh yes, I feel myself warming up to the eccentric women taking me in. I have a feeling this will be quite the adventure.

* * *

The night before my first day of school is an evening filled with different emotions. I'm nervous as could be, and Aunt Rachel's continuous assurances seem forced and empty. This is my one and only chance to start new; different people, teachers, classes, basically everything. Five months ago, I couldn't have cared less about what outfit to wear to school, but now, I'm frantically changing clothes in an attempt to find the perfect ensemble.

Unable to sleep, I toss and turn for a greater part of the night and eventually find myself wandering the small house. The tiny, retro kitchen is well stocked with every kind of food imaginable, so I grab a green apple and return to my bedroom. The room is just to my liking; not too plain, not too flashy, with just enough extra room to transform the space into a comfortable haven.

The one thing I love most about the room is not the large queen bed, (which is so fluffy I had to wonder what the mattress was made of) but the view I have from my window, which can't be more than five feet off the ground. I can see the vast Montana landscape more perfectly than anywhere else in the house, my own personal painted canvas of land.

The view overlooks a valley, the red barn, a pasture and the mountains in the distance, which are spotted with rays of sunlight during the day. On my first morning here, I was woken by Rachel specifically to see the sun rise. It was worth every moment of sleep loss.

I bite into the apple, feeling its sour taste spread across my tongue. Five months ago, I would have eaten the apple robotically, but now, I relish every bite and flavor that hits my mouth. I close my eyes and breathe in slowly, then exhale. Minimally, I feel more relaxed, but not enough to sleep yet. So, instead, I throw the apple core into the garbage can and move to sit on my puffy bed. Honestly, if I never had to leave this bed again, I would be content.

Lying down on my back on top of the plush blue comforter, I close my eyes and whisper a prayer to God. "God, I want to thank you for this chance at a new beginning. I will do everything in my power to make this right again, and I thank you for your faith and strength. Please give me rest," I say quietly, clumsily breaking the steady silence of the room. My prayer every night since I have arrived here in Montana has been similar, but always filled with sincerity and trust.

In the next moment, I'm asleep and having one of those "I know I'm dreaming but there's nothing I can do about it" dreams.

I was walking through the hallway of an unknown house next to a boy I have never seen before, but a voice in the back of my mind screamed familiarity. He had tears streaming down his face, as he burst into a large, empty bedroom.

Without warning, he let out a strangled sob and ran his hands through his shaggy light blonde hair. The boy picked up a maroon colored lamp and flung it across the room with a scream that sent chills up my spine. His face was blurred, as if I was seeing him through a glass of water. He paused, sobbing, and turned towards the bathroom. I followed, a sense of dread filling my entire body, threatening to crush my heart with its hammering presence.

The boy started filing through a cabinet, tears still streaming. He found what he was looking for, which was apparently a prescription bottle. With no hesitation, he unscrewed the tight cap and poured practically the entire bottle in his mouth. I wanted to stop him, but my mouth had no voice. Frozen, I watched him take three large gulps of water from the running facet before reaching for another bottle of pills in the cabinet and repeating the process.

The boy collapsed on the ground, sobbing, grasping at a picture frame I hadn't seen in his hands before. I crouched down on the ground next to him and caught a glimpse of my wrists, which were unscarred. I stood, looking in the mirror at myself in my sixteen-year-old body, short hair and all.

The boy, wearing a green shirt and clutching the photograph of a smiling little girl, started twitching on the ground, and I forced my terrified gaze from my reflection. Kneeling next to him, I saw three people standing around him looking pained. An old man was holding the hand of an old woman and a man in a fire-fighter uniform was in front of them staring at the boy.

"Please, help him!" I begged, feeling a sense of terror as the twitching intensified. "Please, God! Help him!" I screamed, and the three people looked at me before disappearing. I ran my hand through the boys' hair, whispering comforting words through my tears. The boy grew lifeless beneath my stroking hand, and with an aching heart `I watched his last breath slip away into a cloud of green mist…

Chapter 3

I wake with a start, beads of sweat slipping down my face and neck. Looking at the clock, I see that I had only fallen asleep about five hours ago, but I know there is no chance of drifting off again. So, I hop out of bed and pad over to one of the two bathrooms in the tiny house.

Turning on the water in the shower, I strip myself of the sweaty pajamas that cling to me. *It was just a dream,* I repeat to myself. Still, the echo of the boys' shrill cry resounds in my skull like a clap of thunder and I'm unable to shake off the uneasiness. I can't remember much detail about the end of the dream, other than it being frightening and strange. Frustration claws into my skull because I want to remember! Something is significant about the dream, but the details are fuzzy.

I step into the now running water, attempting to wash away any signs of the nightmare, dismissing it as an effect of the ice cream I ate too soon before I went to bed.

About what I judge to be a half an hour later, I emerge from the shower sparkling clean and with smooth legs. My hair has a very natural curl to it, spirals framing my oval face with their caressing flyaway hairs. The great thing about hair is that it always grows back. Slowly but surely, it grows. Looking in the mirror, I finger the cross hanging from my neck and think a silent "good morning" prayer to God.

I open my eyes and see a renewed hope in them, an emotion that still feels unnatural in my body. It's not uncommon for me to feel dulled to the good things around me. That is part of my punishment; the good things are muted, still noticeable, but muted none the less. I wouldn't even know the feelings were subdued without the fuzzy voice in the back of my mind telling me that they were. It is a voice I have grown to trust of late, one that whispers to me things that would normally go unseen. Call it a sixth-sense, guardian angel, whatever you want, but do not doubt the fact that there is someone giving me wisdom.

The voice isn't so much a voice, but more like a very strong feeling grating against my brain until I open my mind and listen. I tell myself it's God, but others would say it's my anxiety medications making me lose my mind.

Through the door, I hear my aunt stirring in the kitchen. Tracing the scar on my left wrist, I sigh and get dressed, humming. Opening the door, which creaks and groans, I use my free hand to adjust my denim skirt so that it hangs more respectively on my long legs.

"Good morning, sunshine! I thought that was you I heard singing in the shower this morning," Aunt Rachel said, winking.

I barely crack a smile through my discomfiture. Singing comes naturally to me and I often do it without even realizing. PANG, the embarrassment spreads through my veins like liquid fire. Quickly reminding myself it is Rachel I stand before, I chase the feeling away by looking out the front window at the mountains. The sunlight casts a perfect view on their tips, making them look like a masterpiece.

"Couldn't sleep late," was all I reply. I wasn't exactly a big talker, a trait that contributed to people's opinions that I'm a snob. That isn't true; I just don't waste words.

A half-hour later, Aunt Rachel, me, and my enormous backpack are packed in the tiny car. It amazes me how at ease I feel around my aunt. Perhaps it's the freeing atmosphere, or her laidback attitude, but whatever it is I'm grateful for it. I know the time will come when she talks to me about my past, my dreams, my hopes, fears, and decisions, but now is not that time.

"Good morning, Sherry. This is my niece, Katherine Mary Prince. Today is her-"

Aunt Rachel gets cut off by the bulbous, alarmingly loud red-headed woman behind the front desk in the principals' office. "First day!" she shouts, clasping her hands together in animation.

"Yes, my dear! We are so excited to have you," the woman says, with just as much verve.

We go through the formalities; the handing out of schedules, maps, locker combinations, and uniforms. Yes, uniforms. The school has a policy that the girls are to wear dress slacks and a polo-shirt or a just-above-the-knee skirt. Being my first day, I'm allowed to dress in normal, casual clothing. I force myself not to wince as I look at the plain gray skirt and maroon polo. It could be worse.

Aunt Rachel gives me a hug goodbye and, with a pat to my backside, sends me out the door of the office. Immediately, I'm in view of several hungry sets of eyes. The school is small, only two-hundred students in the entire institution, and it seems like every eye is focused on me. No, not only me, but me and a terrifying looking boy standing a few feet to my left. I didn't even see him until the prying eyes shifted to him. His face is the only one I can see that isn't focused on me.

Instantly, I'm struck by his beauty. Not a fake type of beauty either, but the kind of raw, natural loveliness that took your breath away. Light-blonde hair that is short enough so that you could see his eyebrows, his black leather jacket covering thick shoulders, and dark jeans that hug his legs just enough to make my heart skip a beat. PANG, the lust flowed through me like I touched a bug-zapper. Blushing, I look down at my new black shoes, trying to calm myself down. How ridiculous, you'd think I'd never seen an attractive guy before.

In that moment, I hear Mr. Beautiful suck in an audible breath. I peek up just in time to see his light blue eyes widen, then dart away from me. Seconds have passed, but they feel like minutes.

"Hey there," a friendly voice calls out from the crowd. "You must be Katherine."

No, not Mr. Beautiful, but a Mr. I'm-attractive-because-I-try-too-hard. Tugging at the corners of my long-sleeve shirt, covering my scars, I answer with a "Yes, hi," which came out breathy, giving me that "new student" awkwardness I wanted so badly to avoid.

The boy smiles, stepping closer to me. Averting my gaze elsewhere, I see Mr. Beautiful push through the crowd of students and into an open doorway. Before he fully enters, he turns back in my direction and catches my gaze, his eyes smiling. With a slightly open mouth, he smiles a barely-there smile before turning into the classroom.

"I'm Scott Persico," said the boy in front of me. I assume he is attractive, in a way. Other girls would be fawning over him, but not me. I prefer Mr. Beautiful types. The lust keeps flowing, and it tastes like bitter pomegranate, my least favorite fruit. This isn't the worst kind of emotion I was punished with, but it was certainly up there.

"Nice to meet you," I say, gingerly shaking his extended hand. Scott's eyes lit up like the Montana sun when my hand touches his. I'm used to being the center of attention and I discover now how much I loathe it.

Scott releases my hand and reaches for my shoulder, but I instinctively step away from his advance. Realizing I probably look like a wounded puppy, I tilt my chin a little higher and stand up straighter, bringing my eyes to the same level as Scott's.

He seems to bristle at the change and his face takes on a confused look. "I'm senior class president, if you need any help with anything at all, just come to me," he says proudly, winking.

He actually winked. Yeah, I'm liking Scott less and less by the minute; cockiness is unbecoming. The crowd of people surrounding us seems to dissipate as our conversation wanes to incessant, forced chatter to fill the silence.

"Well, the class bell will be ringing right about now. Where is your next class? I could walk you there, if you'd like," Scott offers, sounding overconfident

I glance down at my schedule, feeling uncomfortable and vulnerable. "AP Government, room 102, Mrs. Hollis," I say.

Scott's face lights up again, brown eyes brightening. "You're in AP Gov? So am I, second period! We could definitely study together sometime. I'm not in your class, but we get the same work so, if you want a study buddy, I'm free anytime," he offers, voice trailing off, dripping with charm. What ever happened to boys playing hard to get?

Blushing, I say a quiet thank you and turn away from his smiling face. Walking into room 102, which is the room Mr. Beautiful walked in to, every pair of eyes falls upon my flushed face, causing me to color even more. Everyone minus the one boy who made my heart race watches me cross the room as I walk towards the teachers' desk.

Without looking up, the woman says, "Katherine Prince, I presume," sounding bored. She holds out her hand, still not looking up, so I place my white sheet of paper in her palm. I'm supposed to have every teacher sign this piece of paper, confirming I attended their class today.

She signs it, hand moving deftly and steadily, before handing it back to me, finally meeting my eyes. Her dark eyes are small and framed with wire-rimmed glasses, giving her the classic "teacher from hell" look. My stomach drops with nervousness and my heart does a somersault.

Mrs. Hollis waves her thin hand in the air, motioning towards the classroom. "Well, take a seat wherever you please," she says, sounding annoyed.

I scan the room for an empty chair. The only one left is in the very front of the room, directly in front of Mrs. Hollis's desk and the chalkboard. I groan internally, a reflex reaction. Mr. Beautiful is sitting in the back right corner, looking at me with a strange intensity before catching my eye. Then, the corner of his mouth turns up slightly and, even at a distance, I see his blue eyes sparkle.

Something in me clicks, like a switch in my brain just got turned on. Without my consent, my hand raises and gives a steady wave to the blonde boy in the back. I didn't even think about moving it; my hand seems to have a mind of its own. In response to my bold gesture, his smile brightens the room even more, shrouding the surrounding students into darkness. Mrs. Hollis clears her throat and sends a pointed look my way before gesturing to the seat. The class snickers audibly.

My back seems to prickle, like tiny needles are being jabbed in and out at an incredibly high speed. The sensation is not painful, but rather endearing and frustrating at the same time. At first, I wonder if there's something wrong with me, but my heart is singing. Pounding abnormally fast, I can hear it in my ears, drowning out the sound of Mrs. Hollis's sharp voice. The hair on the back of my neck is standing straight up, so rigidly that I can feel it moving with the breeze coming from the window.

Palms sweating, I not-so-subtly turn my head and glance at the dazzling boy who is perplexing me so. I expect him to be paying attention to the lecture, like every studious teenager in the room with us. However, his eyes are fixated on me, the intensity returning with each second our stares hold each other.

"Miss. Prince, may I have five minutes of your undivided attention?" I hear from behind me.

Snapped from my strange trance, I spin around in my chair so fast my earring whips against my cheek and my chair raises off the ground a little. Eyes wide, I feel my cheeks once again fill with blood, the embarrassment hitting me like a ton of bricks. Thank goodness embarrassment wasn't part of my Punishment; otherwise I would be totally screwed. *What a wonderful first impression*, I think to myself.

"I'm sorry," I mouth, fiddling with my fingers in my lap.

To my surprise, the frightening woman actually gives me a small, forgiving smile. "As I was saying," she continues with her lecture until I feel like my ears will bleed and economics will pour out of my nostrils.

The bell rings, and I hesitate while packing my bag. Seeing the photograph of me and my brother in my wallet, my throat closes tight around itself, invisible fingers latching onto one of my many weaknesses. What is he doing right this moment? Why hasn't he answered my last letter? It's been months since I've heard from him. I previously gave him my new address, so he has no excuse. I stare at the photograph for a moment, remembering the feeling of his heavy arm around my shoulders.

The prickles are back, this time on my entire body. I know before I look up who stands beside me, as if my body is a compass and he is north. My heart pumps faster with no provocation and I drag in a quick breath before my lungs cave in.

"Hi," I hear. The sound pierces every pore on my skin, sending a pleasant vibration into every inch of my body. The voice is sexy and deep, but comforting in its surety.

I look up, eyes slowly meeting the blue ones that stare tentatively down at me. Although I noticed, I didn't think about why he wasn't dressed in a uniform. He didn't receive as welcoming a greeting as I did, if he's new.

Up close, I see how strikingly handsome his features are. The semi-short light blonde hair, piercing eyes, and tanned, toned, perfectly clear skin make for a picturesque model of what a boy should look like. Add that to the calmness of his voice, and you'd think a Calvin Klein model walked out of a magazine. His jaw is strong and defined with a perfect nose dotted with freckles.

"Hello," I say, voice shooting up a few octaves, shaking. I mentally chastise myself for being such a *dimwitted moron* at the moment, but keep my friendly face composed.

His eyes smile, but his face remains stoic. "First day, huh?" he says.

That voice… I nod, unable to form coherent thoughts while the tingles turn my skin to ice. I'm uncomfortable feeling so meek just by the sound of his voice, but there is nothing condescending about his tone; maybe I'm going crazy.

"Mine too. Well, first day back," he says, sounding embarrassed but keeping his expression pleasantly neutral. He reaches up like he's about to run his fingers through his hair, but stops and drops his hand, a miniscule bitter smile gracing his lips.

I can feel it rolling off him, the acrimony, as if in waves of sap; the thick, heavy, sticky emotion clings to my sensitive skin, trying to work its way into my system. I somehow find the strength to pull back, willing it away with just a flick of a mental finger. I smile, finally feeling in control once more.

"You went here before?" I ask, putting my books into alignment in my bag, avoiding looking at the picture in my wallet at the bottom. It's buried, out of sight. Just like David.

PANG, the greed and grief starts pumping through my veins, working their way from my heart to every inch of my pathetically human body. I taste them on my tongue, smell their putrid odor in my nose, and feel the banging of their demons in my head as they try to force their way into my mind, attempting to once again steal my sanity. I grip my stomach in an attempt to stop the gagging, but then I feel something else.

A hand rests tentatively on my shoulder, squeezing lightly. The gagging sensation leaves me, along with the emotions that were just coursing through my veins. I look up, stunned, to see concerned blue eyes boring into mine. I feel as if he sees something I don't; as if he's looking into the very depths of my soul and trying to unscramble the mess that was once a thriving young woman.

He is the first to break the silence. "Are you alright?" he almost whispers, instinctively leaning closer. The freckles on his nose are rather adorable and add a refreshing youthful look to this otherwise rugged looking boy.

I just stare at him like an idiot until my body, again, acts of its own accord and nods. He immediately relaxes, the clouded look leaving his eyes as he takes his hand back slowly. I instantly miss the pressure of his fingers, and I find myself slouching before righting it quickly. My father taught me to never slouch, and literally beat it into my head that it was one of the worst, unladylike habits a girl could possess.

"I'm Tristan. Tristan Presidio," he says, offering not his hand, but a stunning smile.

I smile back, unable to help myself. "I'm Katherine. Katherine Prince," I respond, standing and slinging my backpack over my right shoulder. My shirt sleeves ride up, so I quickly tug them back down, hiding my scars.

His eyes take on that knowing look again, and his smile doesn't falter. "I know," he says, voice laced with an unidentifiable emotion. That is strange to me, that I do not recognize it. Determining emotions is something God has made very simple for me, which is both a blessing and a curse. More of a curse, really... literally...

Tristan speaks again, quickly. "I mean, everyone's been talking about you last week. It's not often there's a new student here. Shields Valley isn't exactly a popular place to relocate to," he says, tugging his jacket sleeves further down.

I bite my lip out of habit. It's a nervous tick, something I do when I'm feeling uncomfortable or vulnerable. My name being spewed from peoples mouths' is not something I consider desirable, and Tristan must see this on my face, because he breaks the short silence again.

"I know you're going to be ambushed all day by curious students," he smirks, motioning towards the few students looking at me as they leave the room, "but I was wondering if you'd want to-"

He gets interrupted by Scott's naturally traveling voice. "Katherine, enjoy your first class? No teacher in this whole school is better than Mrs. Hollis," he finishes, sending a wink in her direction. He winks an awful lot. She rolls her eyes and turns back to the blackboard, writing down various things I vaguely recognize.

I am freed from having to converse with Scott by the warning bell that tells us we have two minutes to get to the next class. Turning back towards Tristan, I feel my usual boldness about to reappear. "Where's your next class?" I ask.

He seems surprised, eyes darting to Scott's back before returning to my gaze. "AP English. Yours?"

I smile. "AP English," I say, somewhat flirty. That surprises me slightly; I'm not the flirty type.

Tristan smiles, his cheeks turning a faint rose color, which is just adorable. "Then we best get going," he says, motioning towards the staircase leading to the second floor.

Chapter 4

Walking next to Tristan to English is distracting to say the least. I keep fighting off the urge to stare at him and more than once we're cornered in the hallway by people introducing themselves to me. Only a few acknowledge the boy beside me. Eventually, we arrive at room 213, about three minutes after the bell. Luckily, our excuse makes sense; I got lost on the other side of the school and Tristan dutifully showed me the way. The teacher was fabulous, to say the least.

We take the last two seats available in the room, on opposite sides of the tiny class. Mr. Morrison, the middle-aged, pudgy, upbeat man clearly has the entire class charmed with his presence, and I immediately take a liking to him. We receive our first assignment, which is to write a personal essay about our worst fears, in less than seven-hundred words. I stuff the assignment requirements sheet into my bag, not wanting to think about fears right now.

I take the opportunity to glance around the classroom during Mr. Morrison's lecture; I love English and have already studied Pride and Prejudice, so I'm paying little attention. The students in the room seem to be fixated on the lesson, but I catch the kind eyes of a girl sitting in the seat behind me. She smiles, showing a mouth full of braces with red bands. I smile tentatively back, hoping to make a friend out of the seemingly quiet girl.

Tristan surprises me yet again as the class continues. Not only does he thoroughly know the material, but has very interesting interpretations of major characters. The students in the room seem to be having a difficult time looking at him, which sparks my curiosity. Mr. Morrison seems thrilled with Tristan's knowledge, but it is obvious he's is hesitant to reveal his insight. He seems… almost shy.

I couldn't imagine a boy like Tristan being shy; it went against every single teenage stereotype known to man. His strong build, incredibly handsome face, sweet voice… I feel a flush grace my cheeks as I think about him, so I quickly avert my thoughts elsewhere. I glance up at him once more as the teacher turns the lights off to play us a scene from the movie of my favorite Jane Austen novel.

He's smirking at his desk, eyes closed, head shaking ever so slightly. It would've looked strange to others, but I often find myself doing this when I have a moment of quiet. If I didn't know better, I'd say he was talking to himself, but his mouth moves so slightly I can't be sure from afar.

Without warning, his head snaps up and his eyes survey mine. He lifts his hand slightly and points towards the front of the room where an old television has begun playing the opening scene. I try to look casual, but don't succeed so I just look at the television, feeling out of control again.

Besides, a boy like him doesn't seem the type that would be interested in a being friends with a girl like me; a girl with something to hide, something- someone- to find… a girl who will stop at nothing until she finds what she's looking for.

The lights flash back on before I know it and the students groan unanimously as the blinding fluorescents assault our sensitive eyes. A few minutes later, after some discussion on the accuracy of the scene, the bell rings and Mr. Morrison dismisses the class. My head acts of its own accord and shifts towards Tristan, who is already halfway across the room, heading towards me, looking at his black boots.

"Miss. Prince? May I please see you for a moment," Mr. Morrison says from behind his desk.

Tristan frowns slightly before immediately masking his face again, cutting off any emotion that may be threatening to make itself known. He waves at me and nods his head in farewell and walks out the door, not looking back. The instant longing hits me like an invisible wall, and I rock back on my heels, grasping my stomach.

Walking towards Mr. Morrison's desk, I observe the ridiculous amount of books he has on the shelves on the opposite wall. "Yes, sir?" I say quietly.

His head snaps up, face stunned. "Now Katherine, don't you call me 'sir." Don't make me feel old," Mr. Morrison smiles kindly. "I want to discuss something with you," he says.

"Mr. Morrison, I have already read Pride and Prejudice, so I apologize if you noticed my distraction in class today," I blurt out, not thinking. My eyes widen slightly and I look down, tugging at my shirt sleeves.

He smiles, looking impressed. "I am not concerned with your academic situation, Miss. Prince. I have no doubt that you will be a fantastic student. What I wanted to mention briefly-" he's cut off by the ringing of the warning bell. "Don't worry, I'll write you a pass. What I wanted to mention briefly," he continues, "is that… Well, I am very aware of your previous situation before transferred here. Your secret is safe with me, if it's something you wish to keep private. The faculty was made aware of your… circumstances upon your arrival."

I am mortified. How could I look my teachers in the face if they all thought I was nuts? I came here hoping to start fresh; new people who knew nothing about me. In every sense of the word, a clean slate. Mr. Morrison must see the mortification on my face, or in my suddenly wide eyes, because he jumps right back into lecturing me.

"Katherine," he mutters softly, taking my upper arms in his tiny hands. I flinch, but he grips tighter. "Katherine, you are most welcome in my classroom, anytime you need a place to go. Do you understand? I respect you; I will not treat you any different than any of my other students. You are always welcome to visit me," he finishes, releasing my arms and stepping back.

Honesty was rolling off the man in waves, and I didn't need to be cursed- or blessed- by God to feel it. My throat constricts, and I immediately duck my head, letting my hair shield my cheeks. "Thank you, Mr. Morrison. I promise not to cause any trouble," I say, eerily formal after his speech.

His face looks slightly pained before it evens out again. "Yes, Katherine. I expect wonderful things from you," he says, voice back to his usual cheery tone. "Now, your pass..." he says, scribbling something onto a spare sheet of paper and then handing it to me.

Luckily, my next period is a free one, so there really is no need for a pass. With no teacher to report to, and no wandering eyes watching me, I make my way into the back courtyard, far more lavish than that of any public school I've ever seen. I walk somewhat sluggishly into the garden and sit down on a concrete bench, putting my head in my hands. I haven't been seated but a minute and those strange, yet utterly familiar, prickles start working their way up my spine, raising the tiny hairs that cover my skin.

"Are you stalking me?" a sultry voice says, coming from above me.

Immediately, my gaze shoots up, looking for the source but seeing nothing except the leaves of a large oak tree. Still seeing nothing, I look all around, standing and turning in a complete circle, utterly mystified.

Then, a low thud alerts his presence behind me, and I turn to see Tristan standing in the garden. With the flowers and sunlight surrounding him, he could be standing in Eden. The thought hits me like a massive boulder, literally sending vibrations from my head to my toes, covering my body in goose-bumps.

Why hadn't I thought of this immediately? Was this boy my angel? The angel the Lord himself promised to send to me? But, God said I wouldn't expect my angel to look like an angel, and Tristan is the epitome of perfection, in my eyes. These feelings of peace- these prickles, the ridiculous longing to be close to him- seems so natural, but foreign. It feels as if my body is on autopilot, acting of its own accord and living my life without me really having any say, which I'm not so sure I like.

But, if Tristan is my angel, wouldn't there be some sign? Other than the strange feelings I get around him...? Those could be hormonal nerves, activated by actually talking to a devilishly good looking boy. Having little association with the opposite sex in recent months, I seem to have forgotten what a reasonable reaction to a hot boy is. I've never felt this way around anyone before, not even the one boyfriend I've actually had.

The silence begins to lengthen, and Tristan's brow furrows. "Are you alright?" he says, voice laced with anxiety.

Great…now he probably thinks I'm psycho. Staring at him like an idiot, stop it! "Yeah, sorry," I answer, but to my dismay, it comes out breathless.

He sits down and takes a bite of a green apple, wiping the juice that seeped from the side of his mouth. I notice a scar running along the back of his wrist before he sees me watching and lowers his arm.

"Where were you just now?" I ask, shaking my head in an attempt to clear it.

He smiles a small, sweet smirk that sends my heartbeat into a frantic rhythm. He smiles even more when he answers, "In the tree… you don't have very good eyesight, do you? I was literally right above you and you didn't even see me," he laughs lightly, the sound bouncing through my ears, filling my heart with peace.

I cannot help the smile that spreads across my lips when I respond. "I wasn't expecting to find you lounging in a tree," I reply, sarcasm dripping from every word.

Keep your eyes open, Katherine, because he is not an angel in your sense of the word...

The sentence plays through my head in fast-forward. *Please, God. Show me if this is right. I need you to show me if this is him.* I silently say that prayer twice in my mind, sending it, filled with hope, to Him.

Not a second later do I see the image of a blonde haired boy in my mind; combing through the medicine cabinet, sobbing. Just like in my dream from the previous night, I watch as he swallows the handful of pills before sinking to the floor, clutching a picture frame close to his chest. However, this time I can see his face perfectly. No longer shrouded with a hazy cloud, I can see that it is Tristan, cowering on the floor, tears soaking his hair- which was shaggy and much blonder. This time, the room doesn't fade to black. Instead, I watch a ghostly image of myself kneel down beside him, stroking his hair back from his face as three onlookers watch me sob with him.

I gasp, coming back to the present. Tristan is still sitting before me, not having shifted an inch from his position on the bench. Looking at me, still smirking, his eyes dance. "Expect the unexpected, Miss. Prince. Isn't that what Mr. Morrison told us today? Or where you too busy daydreaming during his lecture," he teases, voice refreshingly light.

I gape at him, mouth open like an imbecile. Well, if I asked for a sign, I guess that was it. It felt like I was in the bathroom with him for hours, watching him sob on the floor. But it must have actually been mere seconds…

Was that the future? Is that what I'm seeing? No, I looked like my sixteen-year-old self in the vision, and it felt like I was watching something from the past, as if my internal clock registered a change in time. He looked slightly younger in the vision, but not by much. Seconds trickle by and I continue to stare at him, trying to comprehend the confusion swirling inside me. I don't want to be confused. I want to understand, to make it better. But what do I know about rebuilding? If anyone needs help, it's me. My mental state is not at its peak, and if my vision was from Tristan's past, then he needs stable people in his life.

Best solution to a problem you don't understand- ignore it and deal with it later, something my parents have taught me well over the years. So, I close my mouth, look away from Tristan, and sit on the pebble-filled ground.

"Don't sit on the ground, Katherine. Here, I'll move over," Tristan says, making room for me on the bench. When my name came from his lips, my body tingled, sending a surprising shiver up my spine.

Wordlessly, I move to sit beside him on the warm concrete, heated by the sun. Its rays hit me in the face, blinding my eyes until I turn my head and the uncomfortable brightness is diminished, thanks to Tristan's head blocking the sun, shielding me.

"Thanks," I say quietly.

"Anytime," he replies. "So, what did Mr. Morrison have to say to you? He's usually the in-your-face type of guy."

"What did you mean? When you said it was your first day back?" I asked, avoiding his question while asking one of my own.

He shifts farther away from me and the blinding sun struck me with its ferocity. Again, he moves, blocking it once more.

"I transferred schools for a while, trying something new," he says with a wave of his hand. "I didn't seem to fit in at the other place, so I came back here," an almost nonexistent chuckle escapes him as he goes quiet again, and I feel reluctance soak through the suddenly thick air.

It is in that moment that I feel his insecurity, his distrust; obviously he's hiding something. Not telling the whole truth and flat-out lying are just about the same thing in my book, and I loathe liars. My entire family has been a lie: the perfect suburban couple, daughter ivy-league bound, the son "away" at a prestigious prep-school.

The façade tires me just thinking about it; that "perfect suburban couple" rarely spent more than an hour with each other a day and they never slept in the same room, let alone the same bed. Their son was not at some swanky prep-school, but rather residing at a boarding school for mentally unstable/troubled youth in Canada. Recently, he got out of that "hell hole," which David liked to call it. His life was on a steep incline as he moved to Los Angeles and began to rebuild himself. His parents, my parents, deserted him when they couldn't deal with his weakness. "His selfishness is unacceptable," I once heard my mother say.

David was anything but selfish. One may argue that suicide is the ultimate act of selfishness, but I beg to differ. Suicide is the easiest way to spare those around you from the heartache of having to live with a person like you in their lives; at least, that's what I once thought about it. The discussion I had with God gave me a drastically changed opinion.

"I'm assuming you dislike your parents," I say boldly. His sarcastic smirk is my answer. "Well, we have that in common."

"Parent, not plural," he states, emotionless.

He looks down at me, blue eyes shining, radiating a type of sunshine of their own. Who needs the sun when his eyes emit such a powerful light? My vision couldn't have been true; this boy in front of me was so strong. His eyes speak a thousand words his mouth does not say; they speak of tumbles and triumphs and sparkle with acumen. These are not the eyes of a rambunctious teenage boy. These are the eyes of an old man, their wisdom adding depth to eyes you felt like you could drown in.

"But, really? You dislike your parents?" he asks, tone sounding genuinely surprised. His emotions, however, gave him away. I knew he already knew this about me- the animosity I felt towards my parents. He was humoring me with his polite questioning and a part of me wonders why he bothers with the pretenses.

"Hey, look! The psycho found himself a new friend," a dark skinned girl called towards us from across the garden, having just walked out the back door. At first, I thought she was talking about me, but then heard the girl say "himself" and realized she must be talking about Tristan. I look at him, confusion knitting my brows together. His face is blank, and other than the slight hardening of his eyes, I would have thought he didn't even hear the girl's harsh words.

She giggles, suddenly surrounded by three other girls and two boys. "Hey, Tristan! Who let you back in town?" a redheaded girl called out, laughing along with the others. I shot them daggers, warning them with my expression to leave immediately.

They all looked at me like I spouted three heads, a subtle expression of shock crossing their faces. "Looks like she's not interesting in making friends," says the dark skinned girl. "Let's go," she turns, the other girls and boys following her back inside the school.

I feel the tingles again and turn my head back to Tristan, wondering what he's thinking. His expression now seems afraid, eyes dull but still reflecting silent panic. "Sorry about them, they're-" he cuts himself off and brushes his hand along his neck.

"I get it," I say, looking for a way to ease him of his weariness. His eyes flash to mine, suddenly filled with unmistakable dread. I feel it invade me, like an unwelcome sickness, drowning me in its syrupy bubble. "There are people like them everywhere, Tristan. The cliché pretty-girl-gone-bad types are easy to spot a mile away," I say in an attempt at lightening the mood, but the words come out heavy and forced.

"It's not that simple," is his reply.

He looks down, playing with a string on the cuff of his leather jacket. Looking at him now, he looks like a bad-boy, the kind preacher men warn their daughters to stay away from. The kind big brothers pummel for even looking at their baby sister. The kind mothers pray their daughter won't show a liking to. Thank goodness none of those people are around me, because there is no way I'm giving up Tristan now.

* * *

Later that night, I'm sitting at the kitchen table, watching Aunt Rachel cook/dance around the kitchen while singing AC-DC terribly off key. The radio is blasting, her feet bare and jeans too tight. What's funny is that I'm actually doing my homework; I haven't done homework in months. I smile at myself and nod my head to the beat of "Highway to Hell," which really isn't a pleasant song if you listen to the lyrics.

I had changed out of my long-sleeve shirt into an oversized t-shirt as soon as I got back to Aunt Rachel's house- another new development. I never wear t-shirts, for fear people might see the thick scars that wrap around my wrists like permanent bracelets, screaming LOOK AT ME, I'M CRAZY.

What I love about Aunt Rachel is her ability to make me feel so at ease. Her carefree spirit makes it easy to forget the troubles surrounding me; she is a complete foil to my mother. How they are sisters is beyond me, with one being so uptight and harsh and the other so spirited and easygoing. It proves blood is nothing more than a human necessity; it holds no real bond between the people it links.

You discover who your family is when they take care of you when you need it. When they look you in the eye and tell you that you're important. Real families don't feel the need to hide their shameful children from the public eye. Real parents don't send their children away because they can't, or don't want to, deal with their child's troubles.

Aunt Rachel would be the perfect mother, if there was such a thing. She is kindhearted, generous in forgiveness, and easy to talk to. She is very young, though; barely thirty-three with her navel pierced and hair bleached blonde. She is beautiful nonetheless.

"Did you meet any cute boys at school?" she asks me as she serves our dinner, a strange concoction of brown rice and various vegetables. It smells delicious, almost like I was suddenly transported to Mexico City.

I smile, thinking of Tristan. I stayed by his side as we conveniently shared every class together except after lunch. Tristan skipped a year in math and had already completed his necessary credits, leaving him with several free periods to do as he pleased after noon. At the end of the day, we parted and my heart fell a little with every step we took away from each other.

"I'll take that as a big fat YES!" Aunt Rachel practically squealed, sounding more like one of the immature teenagers that have surrounded me all day than my temporary legal guardian.

I blush a deep red, embarrassed at being caught. I feel like Tristan should be my own personal secret, but I can't imagine not telling someone about how perfect he is. But that's the thing... I feel like, if I tell people about him, he'll disappear and I'll wake up.

It's like I was born knowing Tristan, and maybe, in some way, I was. If God wills it to be, then it will be. I trust His judgment; trust that He willed Tristan and me to meet. But I wonder if He overestimated my supposed goodness.

A boy like Tristan is much too wonderful to be tempted by a nobody like me, but maybe this proves he is my angel. God said I wouldn't expect him to be meant for me. He was right; if it weren't for the prickles and visions, I would never have thought such a beautiful boy could be mine. The fact that I get to see him tomorrow sends a smile to my face, and Aunt Rachel laughs, this time sounding her age.

"Well, when you're ready to talk to me about him, you talk, you understand?" she says, only half-joking. "Gosh, look at you; first day at school and already blushin' over some boy."

I wonder if she's happy I'm not acting like a crazy person. I can only imagine the stories my mother told her about how unstable I am or how disobedient and entitled I act. Props to my aunt for being so unbiased towards me.

What she doesn't know is that Tristan is not just *some boy*. He is my angel. The insane urge to correct her is almost unstoppable, but I miraculously succeed.

Chapter 5

Three weeks later, I find myself sitting in the garden with Tristan during our free period. He laughs as I tell a story of me and David from happier days. His laughter is light, natural and comforting. The smile on his face makes me feel at ease, and somewhat proud. I, the unlovable nobody, made this beautiful boy laugh. Pride and cockiness swells in my heart, feelings I am a stranger to.

"Who knew you were a rebel?" he jokes, nudging my shoulder with his own, sending prickles up my entire side.

I laugh a sound so unfamiliar it almost scares me. I'm not used to being so open with those around me, but Tristan is undoubtedly my angel. Every night since I met him, I've had flashes of him in my dreams. Some more detailed than others, some make me blush just thinking about, and others were more cryptic. Nevertheless, I am now enraptured with the young man sitting beside me. After three weeks of knowing him, I already feel myself unraveling, but in a good way.

It's been so many years since I've allowed myself to trust. Untying the knots of suspicion does not come easy, but it's much better to face your fears head on. Tristan brings out the old me; the girl that was not afraid of letting others see who she wants to be. The feeling of being completely vulnerable is new to me; I've let myself be impervious for far too long, never knowing what I was missing out on.

In three weeks, I have discovered my ability to forgive. Tristan's unfathomable kindness disarms me frequently, but he is helping me forgive my parents. The best part about this is that he doesn't even realize that he's helping me.

Not complete forgiveness, no; the scars are too deep to forgive anyone completely, especially myself. The wounds run deeper than I have ever thought they would. Not the physical scars of course, although I have plenty of those, too. No, these scars are the ones left carved into my bones, forcing me to cover them with ignorance and avoidance. No more; there will be no more hiding from my demons. It is time I met my fears head-on, and I know just where to start.

The next day, Sunday, I write a letter to my father. In less than a page of my cursive script, I tell him everything I have bottled up since the day he sent David away. Every last hateful thought, every loathsome word mumbled under my breath as he welcomed guests into our home. *Everything* is written in this letter. I never intended to send it, but I do. It's easy, plopping the letter into the cold metal box. It's like discarding a handful of regrets into a fire, never having to feel their sting again. It feels nice, the brief weightlessness I'm given.

Sitting at the tiny round kitchen table, I'm struggling with my Calculus homework when Aunt Rachel walks into the room. "Hey, Katherine, what are you up to?" she says, tone a little too light to sound natural. I wonder what she's up to.

Aunt Rachel and I are closer than I have ever been with my mother. More than anything, she reminds me of an irresponsible big sister I've been forced to stay with while my parents are on some dream vacation. Sometimes, I try to convince myself that that is actually the situation; my daydreaming works most of the time, until I see the thick scars on my wrists, proof that this is reality.

"Calculus," is all I respond, not in the mood for conversation. Keeping my head down, I fumble with the tiny keys of my calculator, threatening to throw it across the room and sending it a mentally silent warning to start cooperating.

Aunt Rachel sits down next to me, brushing her long bangs away from her green eyes. This is one thing her and I have in common; our eyes are the exact same shade of emerald green. I once had a boy tell me they were the most beautiful color eyes he'd ever seen, but my inner-critic told me to shut him out and think the opposite, so that's what I did. That is what I did with everyone, but I'm working on my self-confidence.

"Oh my, I've always hated math, especially calculus!" Aunt Rachel gushed, pushing her cuticles back from her perfectly manicured fingers. I never understood why she acted the way she did in her free time; so flippant and carefree. In reality, Aunt Rachel's job is to be serious. She is the town's only attorney, which shocked me when I came here. It did explain a lot though, like her ability to buy me the newest gadgets and a new wardrobe. I get the feeling that she is extremely modest with her money, which she must have a lot of.

Not saying anything, I nod my head, silently wishing she would leave me alone. Instead, she speaks again. "Why don't you go for a ride today? I'm going to work in a little bit and have a date tonight, so I won't be home until late," I look up, startled she said "date." She winks.

"Go to the barn! You haven't been down there yet to meet the horses. The black one- Dino- is the softest one to ride. Do you remember riding a horse when you were little?" She gushed again, grasping at her chest as if she was in physical pain. If she wasn't smiling, I would've thought she was having a heart attack, the way her nails dug into her shirt.

"I don't think so. And no," was all I said. The silence got suddenly awkward so she patted my shoulder, ignoring my flinch, and left. Moments later, I heard the crappy old car groan to life. When I asked her why she didn't get rid of the POC (which stood for 'piece of crap,') she said it was a classic that belonged to my grandfather and she could never part with it. I had laughed internally, wondering what it would take to make her sell that hunk of junk for parts.

Instantly, a thought flashes through my mind. Tristan gave me his phone number, and while I have a cell phone, I never use it. There is one person in my contact list, and it's Aunt Rachel because she plugged it in for me. I've never been one to embrace technology, preferring books to the internet and television.

Before I lost my nerve, I went into my room and got the phone from the drawer beside my bed. Flipping it open and pressing what I remembered to be the "on" key, I waited for the chiming music to signal me its' powering up. *Ding*, the phone chimed to life.

I opened it and dialed Tristan's phone number, which I had written in sharpie on my hand still. In less than ten seconds, I heard his voice.

"Hello?" he said, sounding annoyed.

My confidence faltered at the frustration in his tone, but I take a steadying breath and force my mouth to open. "Hi, Tristan, this is Katherine," I say shyly.

There is a brief silence on the other end, then a slamming of a door. "Katherine! Hi, uh, sorry about that… How are you?" he said, much kinder and the flutters in my stomach take off.

"It's ok. I'm good, but I'm calling to see if… maybe… you could, I mean, if you want to, come to my aunt's house today and go hiking with me? I've had enough calculus to last a lifetime," I say, trying to sound uninterested.

Again, a brief silence followed. "Sure, that sounds great, actually. What's your address?" he asks, sounding genuinely pleased.

"She lives at 113 Clingsburge Road," I say. "I mean, we live," I correct.

This time, the silence on the other side of the phone is even longer. I wait, but still no response. "Hello?" I ask, feeling foolish.

"Yeah, sorry. Is Rachel home?"

I shake my head and then realize he can't see me through the phone. Rolling my eyes at my stupidity, I say "No. You know her?"

He laughs, sounding light. "You do remember how small this town is, right?"

I laugh too, smiling at the sound of his. "I could never forget. You can come over whenever you want," I say, sounding like a school girl again.

To my surprise, he agrees to be over in ten minutes. We hang up with a casual "see you soon!" and I am in panic mode.

What was I thinking? I wasn't, that's the problem. Maybe I didn't make this decision at all; I've been a big believer in fate of late, as would be acceptable given the circumstances, but terror still shoots up my spine.

PANG! The actual fear hits me like thousands of icicle tips, pricking at my skin with their cold points. I clutch my stomach, warding off the fear with thoughts of David, Tristan's eyes, and the Montana landscape. Before I know it, the feeling is gone, having left a cool, uncomfortable sting behind. There is a knock on the door, sending my heartbeat into frenzy.

I take a deep breath and pull my hair around to the front of my neck to frame my face. Lifting my chin higher and pulling my shirt sleeves down, I open the door. Tristan looks striking in a black button-down long-sleeve shirt hanging open over a white t-shirt that graces his torso while dark jeans and black boots cover his lower half. His smile is the most dazzling of all; brightening his blue eyes and making them shine. I feel my temperature rise and blink a few times, trying to get a grip on myself.

"Good afternoon," he says, voice dripping with happiness but still so sexy. I lick my lips without thinking.

Eyes never leaving his, I say, "You too. Want to hit the trails immediately or have a snack first?" I ask.

He purses his perfect lips, making mine tingle in an unfamiliar way. I bite my lower lip, forcing it to stop behaving so ridiculously. "Why don't we go for a different type of hike… save ourselves the walk," he says, raising his eyebrows, voice suspiciously innocent.

I raise my left eyebrow, showing my confusion. Tristan smiles and laughs at my expression. "Come on, I can tell you need a little peace and quiet," he says, cocky grin morphing into a sad little smile.

Still confused, I shrug, stepping out into the sunlight. I don't care where we go or what we do, as long as Tristan is with me. I feel an unfamiliar sensation in my right hand; one that is sending scream-like signals to my haze-filled brain to reach for Tristan's hand, but I refuse to make him uncomfortable. Besides, I don't want to push him away by alerting him of my strange feelings or conflicting thoughts… being his friend is better than nothing, so I'm content with just being by his side.

To my shock, I feel warm fingers caressing mine, teasing and testing. He's seeing if I'm okay with him holding my hand, and my body responds before I have time to consider the consequences. I lock my fingers with his, smiling as I feel his palm press against my own. From the corner of my eye, I see his lips lift in a discreet smile.

We walk down the front stairs, reveling in the beautiful scenery. Tristan was probably used to the beauty, but I still find myself stunned by the picturesque terrain. Not wanting to break the silence, I let him lead me in the opposite direction of the road.

"Where are we going?" I ask after a few moments of peaceful silence, unable to control my curiosity any longer.

He looks at me with a mischievous gleam in his light eyes, a look I haven't seen before. "For a ride," is all he says.

My footsteps halt, stopping Tristan as well. "I don't know how to ride a horse! Isn't there something less… adventurous that would appeal to you?" I say, attempting to joke, but the serious undertone is obvious.

Tristan just continues to walk, pulling me with him by my hand. Our fingers have stayed locked since we left the house, and I'm in no rush to move them. If riding a horse would force us to separate, I refuse to go along with his plan.

About ten minutes later, we climb over a hill and I see the barn, the closest I'd come to it since I've been here. Suddenly, a question pops into my mind. "How did you know Rachel has horses?"

He raises his eyebrows and slows our pace slightly. "She's never mentioned me?" he asks, voice laced with shock and worry.

Tristan keeps his gaze centered on the ground in front of us, probably trying to avoid any tumbles onto the ground. "No, she hasn't," I answer slowly.

I hear a sound that seems like a grunt, but more like a hum, coming from Tristan. "Well, I've ridden one of her horses- Dino- before. Quite a lot actually. I'm kind of surprised she has never mentioned me," he says, disbelieving.

Suddenly irritated with my aunt for not bringing up the beautiful boy that rides her horses, I force the frustration down and try to enjoy the moment, which isn't difficult to do.

"Her and I are still… coping, with living together," is all I reply. I'd give details if he asked me to; hell, I'd tell him my whole story if I didn't think he'd run for the hills.

He nods, looking deep in thought. "I don't know much about you, Katherine. I get the sense that you don't want to open your life up to everyone, but I'm not everyone. You know you can trust me, right?" I feel him squeeze my hand.

I attempt to smile slightly, but can't. He pulls me closer to his side, so close that our shoulders touch and our legs almost brush together as we walk. I feel instantly calm, ready to tell him anything he wants to know.

The old me would've been mortified to be walking hand in hand with a boy like Tristan; a boy who is not only beautiful, but dangerously compelling. I no longer refer to my ancient happy-self as the "old me"; I refer to the closed off, suicidal, and miserable girl as the old me. Something inside me sings at this revelation, and I'm stunned I have made such progress. I send a silent "thanks" up to the man who made it all possible.

After ten more minutes of leisurely walking, we stand at the open door of the large red barn. The smell is immediate, but I find it oddly homey instead of being repulsed. Tristan pulls me into the structure behind him as he turns his head from side to side, searching.

He gives my hand a squeeze before he releases it. After being hand-in-hand for so long, the cool air on my warm fingers feels wrong and unwelcome. I frown, but turn my face away so he won't see it. I hear footsteps, Tristan's, as he rounds the corner on the opposite side of the barn. I follow him, unsure of what to do.

"Here we go," he says, grunting as he heaves a saddle off the wall. Instead of handing it to me, he slings it over his arm as he grabs a second one.

"Tristan, I wasn't kidding about not knowing how to ride," I say in one last stitch effort to save myself from the embarrassment of potentially falling off a horse. My voice is laced with fear, and I feel it start to prickle up my body, from my toes to the tips of my hair.

Fear is one of the worst emotions I was forced to be overly subjected to. It makes my heart beat uncomfortably fast, and my hands shake. Not wanting Tristan to see my over-reaction, I put my hand to my forehead as I take deep breaths, warding off the encompassing feeling.

To my surprise, I feel a hand grasp my wrist lightly. Immediately the painful fear is gone, replaced with warmth that is lightening. I sigh, loudly. I open my eyes to find Tristan standing close to me, eyes filled with what looks like panic. I'm unsure what to think of this, but then he closes his eyes briefly and when he opens them seconds later, the fear is gone.

"It'll be alright, trust me. You're probably a natural, being Rachel's niece," he says comfortingly. "If you really don't want to, we can do something else. This is the best kind of therapy, though... trust me on this," his eyes beg, tempting me.

Although I should say no, peer-pressure and all, I trust him inexplicitly, so I nod.

"If you're scared, we can share Dino. He's really gentle, my favorite," Tristan says, leading me out the back door of the empty barn. I wonder for the first time where the horses are.

There is a small room in the barn, separated from the stalls and bags of feed and hay barrels. It's more like spare space, having no walls or door. But the tiny area isn't bare; there's a small couch, bed, and a desk by the large window, overlooking the hill we just climbed. The bed looks like the sheets are fresh, but perfectly neat, showing no signs of anyone sleeping in it. Curious… but, then again, Aunt Rachel seems like the type to have a plan-B for any rendezvous she might have.

We exit the barn through two large, open doors and into a beautiful green pasture. The sun glints off the red of the barn, making the color so bright it hurts my eyes. The grass waves in the light breeze, in desperate need of cutting. The pasture isn't large; the fence extending maybe three-hundred feet in all four directions, but the allure is not dimmed by the size. Perhaps I will one day get used to the beauty of this state's country, but I hope it won't be any day soon.

The breeze pushes my hair back from my neck, exposing its pale surface to the blazing sunlight. Emerging from the dark barn into this magnificent sunlight is like awakening from a nightmare, just more real.

Tristan watches my face as I take in the scenery, a small smile playing on his lips. I avert my gaze from the landscape and focus on the horses grazing in the pasture, looking shiny and strong in their element. The black one is the most stunning animal I have ever seen.

"The black one is Dino. Watch this," Tristan says, releasing my hand and holding up the saddle. He jingles a bell that is hanging from the side of the leather patch on the side of the riding instrument, and Dino's head snaps up instantly. He waits for a moment; Tristan jingles the bell again and Dino races towards the gate while the other horses continue with their snacking.

I laugh, unable to hold in the sound of elation. We run over to the gate and I find myself suddenly filled with excitement. Tristan looks at me cockily, which makes my smile wider.

"Trained him myself," he says, unhooking the lock on the gate and pulling me to his side. Backing us up as he pulls the gate open, Tristan makes a clicking sound with his tongue.

Dino walks out of the pasture, head high and trotting excitedly towards the barn. Tristan shuts the gate and, with a gentle click, locks it back into place. He picks up the saddle, which he had set on the ground, and we walk over to Dino.

I'm struck by the grace of the animal; even in stillness, it has a radiant glow that would make anyone awestruck. His black coat, so black it looks midnight blue, is shiny and completely clean; his tail is long and knot-free, and his mane is French-braided, looking beautiful. The horse is possibly the most exquisite creature on the planet.

"Beautiful, isn't he?" says Tristan, lovingly stroking the horses thick, muscular neck. "This braid is really killing his badass looks, though," he jokes.

I revoke my earlier statement; Dino is not the most exquisite creature. Tristan, however, is. I watch carefully as he puts the saddle on Dino with ease, obviously skilled and knowing. Before I can comprehend the deftness of his movements, Tristan is straddled on the secured saddle. He holds out his hand to me, leaning down from atop the large horse.

"Ready?" he asks, face bursting with happiness.

I couldn't have refused in a million years. My knight in shining armor was, literally, swooping me off of my feet and riding away with me into the sunlight. I laugh out loud at the cliché thought, chastising myself for thinking such girlish thoughts.

I grasp his hand and he instructs me on what to do. Placing my left foot in the stirrup, I grasp his hand tighter as my right one clamps onto the saddle, pulling. Suddenly, I'm practically floating through the air, my leg swinging around instinctively and resting on the opposite side of the horse.

"Great! See, I told you you'd be a natural," Tristan laughs, the sound vibrating through him, and I could feel it because I was pressed against his back. My cheeks flush with color and I am glad he can't see my expression.

Tristan flicks the reigns slightly, sending the horse into a slow walk. "Where do you want to go?" my knight asks.

I smile and reply, "Anywhere."

He turns his head so I can see his smile. "Be prepared, it's gonna be a long, bumpy ride," he says with a mischievous tone.

I laugh, giddy with euphoria. The ride couldn't possibly be bumpier than the walk here, but if it is, I know I have Tristan to hold on to.

Chapter 6

He seriously wasn't kidding about it being a long ride. The watch on my wrist told me it has been almost forty-five minutes, and my butt is sore from bouncing on the hard saddle. I wasn't complaining about the ride, mostly because I was stuck pressed up against Tristan.

In these forty-five minutes, we haven't said a word. Not one moment of this time has consisted of any awkwardness, but rather a steady peace that fills me with happiness; real, pure happiness. My angel, my knight, the one to show me it is possible to feel again. The one to show me it is possible to feel such staggering happiness. All this contentment, just from a ride through the woods, with the light streaming through the tall trees like raindrops of sun and the air thick with the smell of pine.

"Here we are," whispers Tristan, just loud enough for me to hear, but quiet enough not the break the spell around us.

I gasp as Dino takes the last few steps towards the edge of the woods. The scene in front of us is truly magical, as if we stepped inside a painting of heaven. For a split second, I wonder if I actually died the day I killed myself, and this *is* heaven. The sun sits lower in the sky, and the mountains, closer than ever before, glimmer with the rays of light being cast upon them. A lake rests at the foot of the cliff-like structure, shining in the sunlight.

"Oh, Tristan," I say, wrapping my arms around his waist even tighter. "It's beautiful," I whisper in his ear, the tickle raising goose bumps on his skin.

He pulls on the rope, stopping Dino in his tracks. Turing his face towards mine, his nose brushes my cheek and my heart stutters. Tristan smiles and pats my hand, which is clenching his shirt.

"This is our stop," he says, shifting. With grace and expertise, he dismounts Dino and stands below me, reaching his hand out, waiting for me.

I take his hand and swing my left leg around and dismount, not nearly as graceful as Tristan, but good enough for a beginner. I smile as I wobble on my numb legs, bending my knees in an attempt to regain feeling.

The pins and needles don't subside as Tristan leads Dino over to a patch of grass, where he promptly decides to lay on his side, basking in the sunlight. I laugh at the sight, never having seen a horse plop down with such finality. It's comical.

Tristan sits down with Dino, stroking his legs and stomach. I'm shocked by his gesture, which is so loving you just know he's done it a million times.

"Tell me how you know my aunt," I say, walking over to the two beautiful creatures. "What's your story?" I ask, unable to help myself. I want to know Tristan, really know him; his past, his dreams, his heartaches. If he's my angel, the least I can do is try my best to be deserving of such a human being.

"I'll tell you mine if you tell me yours," he says darkly, eyes taking on an intense look that frightens me slightly. "You'll hear it anyways," he mumbles.

My heart picks up, unwilling to be unaffected by his words. Telling him my story would mean risking this feeling of perfection. I don't want his curiosity to intrude on my fantasy; my fantasy that everything is normal, that I am not a wounded soul on a mission to rebuild. Revealing my past would mean giving Tristan a free-pass into my future, and part of me is still hesitant to subject him to the horror that was my life.

Picking up on my hesitation, Tristan smiles, but it isn't a kind smile. It's more of a sneer, filled with bitterness and animosity. I'm afraid it's for me, the nervousness and hurt dripping its way into my blood like morphine, but I keep my face schooled. Tristan's expression immediately changes, shifting into a horrified look of disbelief.

He grabs my hands in both of his, instantly freeing me of the worries inside me. His eyes narrow slightly and I see his jaw smart, his teeth clenched. Closing his eyes, he takes a deep breath, and when he opens them, all signs of anger, fear, or bitterness are replaced with a glowing kindness.

"Katherine," he hesitates, looking at our hands. "Do you believe in angels?"

Stunned, my mouth pops open and a cold sweat breaks out across my back, making me shiver. What would sound like a bizarre question to others sounds like a lifeline to me; the final lifeline I need before throwing myself into the ocean. I trust him, and something inside of my heart clicks into place.

"Absolutely," I say, biting my lip as it trembles. His head swivels up, making his eyes level with mine.

"Do you believe in God?" he asks, sounding cautious.

"Even more so," I answer immediately.

"Do you believe in second chances?" he says, sounding hopeful.

"Absolutely," I say, eyes threatening to fill with tears.

"I've waited to hear you say those words for a long time. I'll tell you my story, but only if you tell me yours first. I want to know about these," he says, releasing my hands and pushing up the sleeves of my shirt, revealing my wrists and forearms. In one quick movement, he flips my hands over so the inside of my scarred wrists are exposed.

I instinctively want to snatch my hands back and run away, but I stay rooted in place, trapped in Tristan's gaze.

"Do you believe in angels?" I ask, sounding breathless.

He sucks in a breath, and gives a strangled "Yes, I believe in angels. Yes, I believe in God. Yes, I believe in second chances."

"Good. Then you won't think I'm crazy," I say.

Telling Tristan my story doesn't feel like a betrayal; it feels like a weight is being lifted off my shoulders, as cliché as that sounds. I begin at the very beginning, with David's story.

* * *

The summer I turned ten years old was one of frightening close-calls. I was almost caught kissing Freddie Johnson in the closet during recess, almost caught climbing the tree in the backyard (which I had been repeatedly told not to climb,) and almost caught with the guilt of the not saving my brother's life.

David was sixteen at the time, in his second year at public high school. He was wild and unpredictable, but I cared about him. Even though my parents had their hands full keeping him in line, he was always there to play ball with me. One day, as I got off the bus from school, I noticed he wasn't there waiting for me on our porch, like he usually was. Our parents worked seventeen hours a day, five days a week, so he spent an awful lot of time alone while I was at dance practice.

I ran into the house, backpack banging against my body, waving my math test in the air and screaming "I got an A!" through the house. Immature for a fifteen year old? Yes, but I've always been so bad at math, I needed to celebrate, even if no one cared.

With each silent moment that passed, my smile faded and I started calling David's name. I heard a massive thud from above my head, and I raced up the stairs, dropping my math test in the process.

I looked in his bedroom first, finding nothing. Then my room, also nothing. Finally, I opened the door to my parents' massive master bedroom, finding nothing. I called David's name again as I walked towards their bathroom in tears. I opened the door to see his body on the floor, in the fetal position, an empty pill bottle in one hand, a picture of me in the other.

Screaming, I shook him as hard as I could, yelling his name repeatedly, beating his back with my fists. Nothing happened, and my sobs turned into uncontrollable screeches as I watched my vivacious brother turn into a cold, lifeless statue of what could have been. I ran downstairs, falling down the last few and landing on my hands and knees, tears blurring my vision.

In the kitchen, I grabbed the phone off the receiver and dialed 9-1-1 as I ran back up the stairs. The operator tried calming me down, telling me to go back downstairs and unlock the front door for the paramedics, and then to start CPR. *Don't worry, help is on the way,* she had said.

Five minutes later, I was slamming my palm into David's chest, trying to follow the operators' instructions. Being fifteen with the body of a ballerina, I hadn't had the proper strength to do compressions correctly, so I improvised. David was breathing, but barely. The paramedics ran up the stairs and into the bathroom, one carrying me away while the others did all sorts of things to David's unresponsive body. Then I blacked out.

A year later I transferred from public school to private school. My brother was sent to "The John Adams Developmental Facility for Traumatized/Disturbed Adolescents" in Canada, and I hadn't seen him since. Other than a letter once every other week, we had no contact at all. The letters were sneaked; David's friend would give them to me when he saw me walking home from school every day, and I would stuff it in my backpack.

You'd think the near-death of a child would make parents motivated to change, but my "parents" seemed completely indifferent to their son attempting suicide. The notebook that was sitting open on the counter was filled with two pages of his reasons for killing himself, and one page was an apology letter to me, but it was illegible.

No one, especially not me, knew what David was going through; at sixteen, he had been drunk at a party and gotten an eighteen year old pregnant. Because the girl was eighteen, she was afraid of getting charged with rape, so she had the child aborted. David found out about his would-have-been child during a fight at school, in which a fellow student of his screamed out that he was a "punk-ass baby-making killer," which made David slam the boys head into the gym floor, giving him a concussion and broken teeth. My brother has always had anger issues, but that was the day everyone found out.

Not only was he coping with this drama, but he was now being incessantly bullied and teased in school for various reasons. Some rumors about him were true, others completely false, but even he couldn't tell the difference anymore. David began using drugs, sneaking our parents' Valium one tablet at a time. Then the time came when he was pushed over the edge, by no one other than our father himself.

A stern man with no conscience, our father was a firm believer in "spanking" sense into his children. After getting expelled from school for fighting, Father brought David home and pushed him into the kitchen wall, hard. I was upstairs, but I heard the door close so I ran to see what the commotion was.

I saw our Father hit David repeatedly with a spatula; a weapon of convenience. David was crying and I had never seen him cry. Not like that. The man we called father was beating David into unconsciousness, and I became terrified for my brother. I charged into the kitchen, grabbed my father's arm and yanked as hard as I could. He whirled around, smacking me across the cheek with the spatula, leaving a sharp sting that spread over my entire face.

"If you EVER screw up as much as this your brother, I will kill you before you have a chance to blink an eye. Do you understand?" the man screamed, following his decree with obscenities.

David wrote an apology letter addressed to me, which I still keep inside my lock-box. I don't know why I keep it; it's too strong a reminder of my brother at his worst. He's growing now, changing into a better person and accepting his past. I admire his strength, his courage to fight his demons head on.

* * *

A half an hour into my story, Tristan reaches towards me and pulls me to him. Together, we lean against Dino on the grass, my head on Tristan's chest, his head on Dino's side. The trust he has in this animal is frightening…

"Katie, I didn't mean to make you cry," Tristan whispers, voice wavering.

I don't want him to be upset; I need him to be strong. My angel deserves to know my story, and I am telling it to him in all its gory truth.

"You didn't, Tristan," I say, sniffling. I snuggle my face into his neck, breathing in the smell of… home. He tightens his arms around me, giving me an anchor to hold onto, urging me to continue, but not wanting to push me too far. I figure I may as well push as far as I can.

* * *

I turned seventeen on July 4th, 2012. That night was supposed to be the best night of my life, but it was the worst I could have ever experienced. The day went as expected; calls came from friends, cards clogged the mailbox, and my cell phone and Facebook wall buzzed with empty birthday wishes from people I haven't talked to in a long time.

The night, however, was anything but expected. I had been driving to the bowling alley with my kind-of-boyfriend, Chris, when he suddenly pulled off the side of the road and parked. Confused, I looked over at him, just as his mouth met mine. The wheels turned in my head as I attempted to process what he was doing, but then I felt his hand glide up the front of my shirt, and I pulled back.

We had a heated argument, which escalated into a full blown screaming match. I wasn't willing to give him anything, and he expected me to because I was a year older than I was when we started "dating." I slapped him, he yelled in my face that I was a teasing whore and a prude, and then I got out of the car and stomped home, but only after slinging vicious words his way, efficiently ending our pathetic "relationship."

It took me almost two hours to walk home, and it had begun to rain substantially hard. By the time I walked through the door, I was soaked to the core and my teeth were chattering. No one was home, so I took an hour long shower before crawling into bed, wrapped in a bathrobe, crying. I stayed awake for hours that night, simply staring at the ceiling.

The next morning, my parents were sitting at the kitchen table, which was a first because they're usually gone by the time I wake up every day. My mother looked upset, my father looking impassive. In less than three minutes, they proceeded to tell me that Chris had died in a car accident the previous night, on his way home from my birthday party, which I didn't even go to. He had a blood alcohol level of .2 and wrapped his SUV around a massive tree near the creek we stopped at. His car was found smoldering at two o'clock in the morning, his body ejected and lying fifteen feet from the crash, slicing in half.

That school year went by in a blur, nothing eventful happening. My life was completely boring, but had been on a gradual slope downward since the night of my birthday. My grades dropped, (not drastically, but enough,) and one by one my friends began to disappear. Not literally, but they became angry with me for becoming such an unfeeling amoeba, and they left me alone to deal with my demons. Every day I was told how worthless I was, how I would never amount to anything, and how I was turning out to be just like my brother.

The final nail in my casket, after being empty for so long was the night I watched my father strike my mother with a bat. He hadn't seen me in the hallway, creeping from my bedroom to get a glass of water from the kitchen, but I saw him. It was a mutual understanding in our family to pretend like everything was normal; like we didn't have fights about my well-being or watch each other get pushed down by my father, mentally and physically.

I attempted to kill myself the next day, using my fathers' pocket knife to slice my wrists open. If you asked me why I did it, I'd be completely honest and say that I was simply done living. I wasn't living, so I guess you could say I was simply done being a zombie. I wanted out of this thing people called life, and I wanted it as fast as possible.

I wrote David an apology letter before I spilled my own blood, in the same type of notebook he wrote his goodbye letters in. Unlike him, I gave no explanation to my parents for my decision. I remember doubting that my parents would even give David the letter, mostly because they hadn't talked to him in years. He was like a phantom; present in our lives for so long, but gone long enough to seem like a ghostly apparition; his face was removed from the house, photographs taken from every frame and hidden away from the world like a secret that must be kept private.

* * *

My throat is becoming hoarse from talking so much for so long, and I haven't moved from my position in Tristan's arms since I began speaking. I take a deep, shuddering breath and finish my speech with a lame "and, now I'm here."

A heavy silence follows, shrouding the peace in a feeling of discomfort. I shift, wanting to see Tristan's face, to see what he's thinking; but his arms tighten around me and I cannot move an inch. This should frighten me, but the gesture feels caring instead of menacing.

"Are you going to say anything?" I say after a few minutes, unable to stand the silence any longer.

He takes a deep breath and sits up, moving both of us into a sitting position. I move away from him, turning my whole body to face him head-on. To my surprise, and pleasure, I find myself looking into awestruck eyes instead of pitying ones; there is nothing I hate more in this world than accepting pity and hand-outs from others. I want them to know I'm strong enough to get by on my own, and I have too much pride to take pity gracefully.

Tristan takes my hands in his, fingers brushing the scars on my wrists, sending an unnatural tingle up my spine that feels like hamsters are crawling their way up my back. Without speaking, he lifts my hand to his mouth and kisses the inside of my wrist, right on my scar.

I feel a tear slip down my cheek, cool and wet on my sun-warmed face. Seeing this, Tristan drops my hands and slides closer to me, taking my face in his hands. I again see the scar that travels up the side of his forearm, and I can't help touching it, running my fingers along its slightly-raised surface.

"I knew it was you," is all he says, a ghost of a smile playing on his lips.

Confused, I tilt my head to the side and raise my eyebrows slightly.

"There is a reason I asked you those questions, Katie. I think there's something you left out of your story," he whispers, leaning closer.

I think he will kiss me. I wait, hopeful, as he leans closer, hands gently squeezing my face tighter. He lays his lips against my forehead, hovering there for a moment before pulling back and looking into my eyes.

"I told you everything you need to know," I answer, breathless.

Tristan smiles sadly, nodding his head. I cannot imagine him knowing about my Encounter with God, and there is no way I would willingly give him that information. I don't doubt he would believe me, but if he is my angel, then I want him to realize it on his own. Also, I feel like the meeting with the Lord was for my eyes only, and it will be a secret just between the two of us.

"It's your turn," I say, wanting to hear his voice.

"Katherine, it's been-" he begins to say, but I cut him off.

"No excuses. If I can open up, then you owe me that much, Tristan," I counter, sounding forceful and immoveable.

He purses his perfect lips, speculating. "Alright, but on one condition," he raises his pointer finger to emphasize. I smile slightly and nod. "I will tell you my entire story if you swear you tell me the rest of yours."

I look at him with an accusatory look. "That was not our deal!"

Tristan raises his eyebrows, "This isn't a 'deal,' Katherine! These are our *lives* we're talking about, here. What type of relationship do you think we can have with half-details? Not the kind I want," he laughs the sound devoid of any humor.

I bite my lip at the word "relationship." Certainly he means friendship, right? But he's acting like he's expecting more. That's right; they always expect more, the tiny voice in my head sings as I think.

"Katherine, I want you to trust me. I trust you! I need you, and you need me; I know you know what I mean, too!" he says loudly, disrupting my inner-battle.

Stunned, I look at him wide-eyed. I attempt to transform my shocked expression into one of innocence, but fail.

"I've waited *two years* to have this conversation with you, Katherine. There's nothing I'm holding back," he continues, eyes fierce.

Two years? I just met him! What does he mean, two years?

Seeing my confused expression, Tristan sighs. "Katie, come on," he pleads, eyes suddenly dark with pleading. "Is this your way of you telling God you want another angel?" he asks accusingly, disbelieving. He shakes his head, a smile forming. "That's not how it works, sweetheart."

My face is frozen in shock, mind unable to comprehend what he's saying. Without giving me time to process his words, he continues. "So, here's my story," he begins, pulling my frozen form down beside him on the grass.

Chapter 7

Tristan

Katherine is more than I could have ever hoped for. I wasn't expecting her to open up as fast as she did; I was actually prepared to beg for months for her to get to trust me. Although, she hasn't confided in me totally just yet, but that's understandable. I pull her down to lay on the warm grass next to me, my arm resting around her shoulders, keeping her head from laying on the hard ground.

The moment I saw her on our first day of school, I recognized her face. Everyone else just knew her name, but I knew something no one else did; her story, on a very personal level. I asked her to tell it to me because I wanted her to know she can trust me, but I know as much as she does- if not more- about her past. We lay there, watching the lone puffy cloud pass over the afternoon sun, which was beginning its descent.

There is no need to ready any courage; when I told her I have been waiting two years to tell her my story, I wasn't exaggerating. These years have been filled with anxiety, hope, and longing, all amplified into extreme magnification. I felt like an ant on the sidewalk, having the light slowly fry me to death as a boy held a magnifying glass over my body. But, the light wasn't from the sun; it was from my past.

I was seven years old when my grandmother died in a freak accident involving a lightning storm; she was struck while standing on her porch, calling me, telling me to get back into the house. I was terrified, so I stayed huddled under the sycamore tree in the front yard, unwilling to move. I watched her fall to the ground, head banging against the wooden floor of the porch, and I saw her not get back up. Staying under the tree, I wept until my grandfather got home.

I had just turned ten years old when my father died; he was a firefighter and killed in the line of duty, attempting to rescue a six-year-old girl who was hiding in her closet. He dangled her out the second-story window before dropping her, twenty feet to the ground, as the house caved in and he was buried in a pile of fire and ash. I watched him die through the footage that played live on the news. My mother became a zombie.

On my twelfth birthday, I watched as a man jumped to his death from the Brooklyn Bridge, landing in the water below us with bone-shattering force. My mother took me to New York as a present, but I left feeling haunted by the man's dead eyes. I will never forget the icy feeling that laced through my body as I watched him jump, and I can feel it to this day, every morning I wake drenched in sweat from a nightmare that replays the event.

For three years, everything was good. Great, even. My mother had a steady job, my sister was over her pre-pubescent hormone fits, and my grandfather moved in with us. My sister, Skylar, is everything to me. Was everything to me... I cared for her like she was the most precious thing in the world, and for an eleven year old, she was pretty easygoing.

Every day, I would walk her to and from school, and then pick her up after football practice at four-thirty. She would never object; on the contrary, she would race down the steps of the school and jump into my open arms on most days. Others, she would simply grab my hand and swing our arms as we walked.

Skylar was my best friend, my baby sister, and my whole world. I would sit through hours of tea-parties, hair and makeup days where she would put a whole tube of gel in my long hair, making it stick up in all directions. I would walk her to the park where we would fly kites and chase each other with water balloons. I would take her to the pet store where we would play with the dogs and cats that weren't being adopted, even though we could never take them home because our mother was very allergic.

My mother was also clinically depressed, smiling when necessary and encouraging us to leave the house often, but leaving me to raise my sister alone. She never wanted us to see her break, but I was old enough to see the signs. One day, I had to physically pour every drop of alcohol we had in the house down the drain. While Skylar and I were at school, she would be home, drinking, and we thought she was working.

My mother was laid off from her job at a foreclosure company, forcing her to take a "temporary leave" with very little pay. With the money she did have, she began to spend frivolously, leaving next to nothing for bare necessities. She became much less "mom" and much more "mother." Our grandfather did everything possible to keep her from falling apart, but the day I came home from a camping trip and found her sprawled on the couch, naked, next to a random shady-looking guy and a whiskey bottle, I had had enough.

I grabbed whatever clothes I could fit into my backpack, and one-hundred dollars from the emergency fund- which was selfish of me- and ran out of the house, car keys in hand. I had my license for barely a month, but I was so lost in a fit of rage I didn't care. Slamming the car door, I saw nothing but red flames of anger pulsing behind my eyes and the wide, open highway that stretched in front of me.

In the oblivion I slipped into, it was easy not to notice Skylar climb into the back seat. In the corner of my mind, I felt her tiny fingers wrap around my shoulder, but I threw them off, fighting the tears that threatened to trickle down my cheeks. I had had enough of our mother, and in my despair, I was accelerating towards eighty miles an hour.

Barely five minutes into my drive is when it happened; a Ford truck lost control and spun in my direction. Frozen, I stared as the hundred-thousand pound piece of metal continued flying towards the side of my vehicle. My foot couldn't find the gas pedal, and I found myself coming back into my body. Anger completely faded, I noticed Sky in the car for the first time. She was looking at me, eyes wide, not seeing Death barreling towards us.

The last thing I heard was her scream before everything went black. One week later, I woke from the coma in the hospital, feeling scared and alone. No one was visiting me, but there was a lone card on the desk next to me. It wasn't signed, so I couldn't tell who had left it here. The doctors told me that I was lucky to be alive; that the car had been so destroyed that the "jaws of life" were used to get me out.

Then I remembered Skylar. Frantic, I started to interrupt Doctor Colson's spiel on how lucky I was and how his quick thinking saved my life. My head was thumping, and he urged me to lie back down, but I refused. The doctor was too pleased with himself to feign sympathy for my condition, so he left the room in haste, sending in a young nurse that had a tattoo on the side of her neck. I remember thinking about how wrong the ink looked on the kind woman, but her next words shattered everything insignificant in my brain.

I killed my sister. Baby Skylar, so young, so full of life, was lying dead in the ground because of me. Hell, I wasn't even at her funeral! That explains why my mother isn't here; she probably never wants to see me again. I remember feeling no pain, no shock;

I remember feeling nothing at all. Simply numb, I lied down on the hard bed in the hospital, staring at the holes in the ceiling tile, counting them aimlessly.

Two months later, feeling hadn't yet returned to my left leg, or my brain. I walked around in a shell, completely cut-off from the person I used to be. The scars on my body were already beginning to fade, but those in my memory were as fresh as ever. I remember thinking to myself, "She's dead. You killed her. It's your fault entirely," over and over again, but feeling nothing.

They say people grieve in different ways, but I would have preferred to be a sobbing mess of a boy instead of being the empty cloud I was. Literally, I remember nothing in those two months. I passed every test I took in school, but retained none of the information. My "friends" were no help or comfort, and the only thing I had left in this world was… nothing.

My hopes, my dreams, my thriving ambition all died that night Skylar was plucked from my hands. She was gone, and our mother soon followed. Not in the literal sense, but my mother became an even more distant stranger when Skylar died. From the outside, we seemed like a struggling family; on the inside, we were already broken beyond repair.

This is the time I spent with Rachel. She took me in, helped me get off the drugs I clung to like a baby. She helped me dump the nameless, faceless girls and try to find my way again. But I never was able to on my own.

I decided to end my soulless existence on July 4th 2010. Now, it seems like a foolish mistake; "a permanent solution to a temporary problem," they say. At the time, it seemed like the easiest way to avoid the unavoidable. Everywhere I looked, Skylar's presence screamed at me, "Why did you do this? Why are you so selfish? Wasn't my life important to you?"

Her bedroom remained untouched, like a tomb of sorrow in the middle of our house. Her school pictures remained on the walls, her drawings on the refrigerator were collecting dust and becoming shriveled, and her closet was still filled with the dress-up clothes we played with so many times.

I had come home- from where, I don't remember, - and found my mother's car gone and the house eerily silent. At one time, there would have been a dancing little girl bounding around the living room, calling my name before running into my arms. I can almost see it for a moment until her ghostly memory fades from my mind.

I used to be able to tell you exactly what she looked like; every freckle on her pixie face, every miss-matched pair of socks in her closet... But with time, my memory faded, and I found myself slowly cracking. *This is what you need, Tristan. You need some closure*, my mind sang, but I didn't want closure.

I wanted Skylar. I wanted my grandmother, my father, my mother back, my *life* back. Waiting for the dead to be reborn is like waiting for snow to fall in the Sahara; a fruitless, pointless effort. I didn't want to feel. I didn't want to be unfeeling. I didn't want to be at all. The decision was made unconsciously, like all my decisions were those days.

Walking up the stairs, I grabbed Skylar's photo off the wall, and that is when I broke. I didn't just break, I shattered. The unfeeling glass wall that was my soul exploded, but I tried to force it back, afraid that regaining feeling again would weaken my resolve. With each step I took, I felt the crash of emotions overtake my body, turning a depression-ridden, wreck of a man into a blubbering mess of a boy.

Our tea parties, cookies at grandma's, her laughter, my laughter, mom's laughter, dad's smile, grandpa's hugs, my lacrosse career, Skylar's singing, mom dancing with dad, me dancing with Skylar... Skylar, Mom, Dad, Grandma, Grandpa... dead, dead, dead, dead...

My heart broke, pouring out sorrow as if it were physical blood. I screamed, filling the house with the horrible sound until I reached my destination; my moms' bathroom. I paced, letting the despair fill me more, as a punishment to myself. A punishment for killing my sister. A punishment for not coping with her loss. A punishment for losing myself when I was supposed to be strong.

I opened the cabinet and pulled out my mom's bottle of prescription pills, poured them in my mouth, and chugged water to chase them down before I lost my nerve. I took another bottle out and repeated the motions, tears streaming down my face. Unable to control it any longer, I lied down in the cold, tile bathroom floor and waited for Death to find me.

My eyes sprung open, and I found myself sitting on the edge of the bathtub. Looking at my hands, I saw that the scars from the car accident were gone; the long, snake-like one that once ran up my forearm had disappeared. I smirked, pleased that I was once again unmarked.

"Tristan," said a voice I couldn't place, but sounded vaguely familiar. Looking up from my fresh hands, I saw a tall man standing beside… me. My eyes grow wide, realization flooding my mind. I'm dead. I killed myself. Now what?

"Tristan, do you realize now how foolish you have been, son?" The man continued, looking at me with such disappointment that I feel the need to bow my head.

"You had so much in store, Tristan. I would ask why you performed this act, but I already know. You and I are not as close as we should be," he continued.

For a flash of a moment, I wonder if the man is my father, but he looks nothing like the man who perished in the fire all those years ago. Confusion settles in, twisting the world into a contorted mess.

"Who are you?" I asked, my voice deeper than it had been when I was alive, which shocks me.

"You should know that, Tristan. You do know. Who am I?" he asked, holding his arms out to his sides.

My mouth opens of its own accord, voice escaping through my lips. "God," it said. Mouth snapped shut, my eyes widen, hand flying to my throat in surprise.

God smiled, and I felt a peace flow through my heart. Around his head rested a halo of green light, and his entire body seemed to be emitting a strange green glow. With long blonde hair, styled like mine was, his blue eyes were kind and inviting. His clothes were the only thing that would signify him as from a different era, a different country. The white robe he had was dotted with green specks, and his bare feet seemed to barely touch the ground as he stepped closer to me.

"Yes, Tristan, you do know me. You also know that you have made a mistake," he says, walking towards my body lying on the floor, crumpled into a ball. "Do you feel that, my child? Your mistake?" he asked, looking up at me.

I *did* feel it. My *soul* felt it; that it was not right for me to be standing here. It wasn't my time to die, and it wasn't my decision to make. It was His; He gave me life, and I foolishly took it away.

I began to feel like I was choking, so I opened my mouth, but nothing came out. I began to grow panicked, but God looked unalarmed. Without warning, black smoke rose out of my throat and wafted through the air like mist, hovering for a few seconds before making a rapid descend towards the floor.

An enormous weight lifted from my heart, and I began to see something playing behind my eyes. They fought to close, but I refused to look away from the man standing before me.

"Close them, Tristan," he said calmly, walking towards me and placing his hand on my head.

I closed my eyes, but they still saw. A scene played behind my lids like a movie, and I watched with fascination. A beautiful girl with blonde hair emerged from a doorway, a look of pain and extreme sorrow painted on her face. She set a notebook on the counter before turning around and pulling off her shoes. Suddenly, she walked towards a bathtub and calmly turned on the water, which was so hot the steam floated to the ceiling almost immediately.

I saw myself in the mirror, standing beside the girl in the bathroom. She looked at our reflections for a moment, and I could see the dullness in her sea-foam-green eyes; a dullness that told the story of a tortured soul. The pain in them made me ache, and I reached forward, trying to touch her, to console the beautiful girl. She pulled a small pocketknife out of the drawer and climbed into the bathtub, fully clothed.

Wincing, I was forced to watch her slice her wrists open, cutting so deep blood spurted out and dropped into the bathwater like food-coloring. She didn't cry out, she simply watched with a bored expression as her blood left her veins. I reached out, wanting to help her, but my hand hit the notebook that was resting on the corner of the sink and it fell to the floor with a thwack. Time passed and eventually she looked up, eyes hazy and face drained of color; I stood there, helplessly watching the girl die in front of me.

"Is this what you want?" says God, who appeared right beside me. He gestures to the girl in the tub, each word hanging in the thick air like the steam around us.

A tear slipped down my cheek as I watched the girl's eyes close. "No! No! I want to help her! I need to help her! Please," I beg, beginning to cry harder as the bath water began to darken further. I stumble over to the side of the tub, wanting to vomit at the amount of blood that was leaking from the girl's wrists. "Please," I whisper, sobbing. *I need to help her, she needs me*, my soul shouted. *I need her, she can't leave. We weren't meant to end like this; not separated so soon.* "Please!" I scream.

The bathroom disappears, and I'm in an unfamiliar living room. There is a man and a woman arguing. Shouting at one another and I can only make out bits and pieces of conversation. Someone named David, someone named Rachel, something about Canada, something about stupidity and wanting a new life. Then the woman shouts something back, but I don't understand what she's saying, because I'm watching the blonde girl cry. She's younger here, maybe fifteen years old, but there is no doubt it is her. An ache in my gut tells me it's her.

The man strikes the woman across the face with something, and the girl runs into the room, flailing her arms. The man strikes her, and she falls down. Then the scene changes again, and I am sitting in the backseat of a car, the blonde haired girl in the front passengers seat and a stocky, dark haired boy in the drivers' seat. He makes my stomach churn. I am forced to watch as he kisses her, and I want to rip his arms off his body. *"Get away from her,"* I said aloud, but it was lost in the lyrics of the song playing.

The girl shoves the boy away and he slings shameful words at her, instantly bringing tears to her eyes as she flees the car. Instead of following her, I remain glued to the seat, watching the boy as he proceeds to drive to a party, get drunk, leave, and then turn the car into scrap metal. His dark eyes remain open, even in death.

Immediately, the scene changes again, and I see flashes of images. It's like I'm being sprayed with a hose of memories; pictures and moments untouched by time as they wheel out before me. Laughter, tears, emptiness, and loss fills me to no end, and I clutch at my chest to stop the pain. I see words, surrounding me, filling my head with their giant letters.

I hear a sweet voice whispering in my head, "greed, jealousy, hatred, lust, bitterness, grief, fear, shame, blame, regret, remorse, apathy, refusal…" The words cross my vision in an orderly array, branding themselves into my heart for eternity.

"Tristan," I heard my name being called, and my eyes flung open. I fell against the wall, gasping, in my own bathroom once again. "Tristan, you are not supposed to be here right now, son. This is not your future," says God, pointing to my body on the floor. "Katherine is your future, Tristan. You can feel her, can't you?" he asks.

Something I hadn't felt before begins to fill me up from the inside out; a fire, burning my chest as it tries to rake its way outward, flooding my veins. It's extremely uncomfortable, so I release my hold on it and let it fill me. An image of the blonde girl flashes in my mind, and I feel at peace for a moment. Then, God places his hands on my shoulders and the girl is gone. *Katherine,* her name is. I feel her inside of me, her light burning, her heart beating and her feelings.

"She needs you as much as you need her, Tristan. You are not only hurting yourself, but hurting her, too. Without you, she won't survive. You see, Tristan, every one of my children has a protector, an angel sent to this Earth to make them happy, to make them strong. You were blind to this fact, Tristan, as are all the others. If you wish to return to your earthly body, you may have a second chance," he says, pausing.

"Please," I beg, falling to my knees. I need this angel- this Katherine- in my life. I need my life. I need her to heal my soul. "I am sorry, Lord. Please, I need this," I say, feeling despair fill me.

"You need to accept my will; without it, I will not let you return," God says. I nod, feeling a lightness fill me as he smiles. "Tristan, this act will not go un-punished. You defied me; turned your back on me when I could have helped you. You will search for Katherine, but you will find her wounded. Your Punishment requires you to face the reciprocations of your Earthly actions. Also, your own feelings will be dulled, but you will feel Katherine's, and hers will be heightened. Her fate is sealed, Tristan. You have watched her kill herself, and you will have to feel her struggle to stay together.

"Because you accept my will, Katherine shall live. The vision I showed you, of her death, is from the future; two years ahead of our time. Until then, she will feel what you should have been feeling for the past two months, for she has been punished as well for her future act of defiance. When you feel your emotions returning, that is when you should pay extremely close attention to those around you. Tristan, I am a loving God, but turning your back on me is the most wretched kind of blasphemy, and this is your Punishment. This is what you need to heal your soul. This is what you need to make things right," he finishes.

I wasn't sure whether to cry or jump with joy; she's safe, I'm safe, we both get second chances. I was still confused, not quite grasping the information being hurled at me, but nevertheless I was elated at the fact that I would return to find her.

* * *

I stare at Katherine's shocked face, not sure whether to say something or just shut up. She makes the decision for me as tears pour from her eyes, spilling onto her pale cheeks and dripping off the sides of her face. About to open my mouth, I watch as Katherine sits upright and buries her face in her hands, releasing a sob so fierce I feel an ache in my stomach.

"Katie?" I say, sitting up and moving to face her. No response, just heartbroken sobs. "Katherine?" this time, I try grasping her hand, but she pulls away from me and my heart drops into my stomach. Did I unload too much on her? Too soon? Desperate for her to acknowledge me, I say, "Please don't cry. I'm so sorry, I didn't mean to-"

She cuts me off with a look so disbelieving it shocks me. "You think I'm mad at you?" Katherine shakes her head, tears flinging off her cheeks like salty rain. "I can't believe you- you would think that," she lets out another sob, covering her face with her hands again. Before I have time to say something else, she sits up straight, hands traveling forward and grasping my face.

"You are forbidden to ever think I am upset with you again! Unless I tell you, physically say to you 'I'm upset with you,' I never want you to even think I am anything but grateful," she says, green eyes locking me in a trance. "I cannot fathom how you-" she breaks off crying again, then closes her eyes and regains her stability. "I cannot fathom how you dealt with feeling my pain. You're so strong. You had to wait so long to feel better. I only waited a fraction of the time you had to," she finishes, hand brushing through my hair before falling into her lap.

I am at a loss for words. If Katherine isn't upset with me, then she must believe me; I knew she would. She's such a fighter, but is truly consumed with self-loathing. It's gotten better in the past two weeks, even more so with help from Rachel. I can't tell her that part of my story, the part I know she won't want to know, because the sun is sinking lower and lower in the peach sky and we should be heading home soon. There is always tomorrow, after all. The thought brings a blinding smile to my face.

"Tristan," Katie whispers, and then pauses for a minute. "Can we head back? Before I pass out from information-overload," she attempts to joke, but I can hear the seriousness behind her words.

I stand, and reach down to take her hand. "Absolutely," I say, pulling her to her feet.

A beam of the setting suns' rays settles on her face, and I see her green eyes sparkle, something they can't do in the dark. I had wanted to get everything laid out on the table, so to speak. Today was going to be the day where she discovered everything about me; not just the detrimental things, but the insignificant things that make a human a person. The information I'm keeping secret, for now, will pop the bubble that I feel so secure in.

She keeps her fingers intertwined with mine as we walk over to Dino, who is grazing by a patch of berry bushes. I walk right up to him, unwillingly releasing Katherine's hand and pull myself up. Scooting back, I lift her slight frame up with no struggle at all, and she is sitting in front of me on Dino, legs straddling the saddle.

We ride the first half of the ride in silence, which is awkward, unlike the quiet from our earlier trek. With Katherine not touching me, I feel on edge and guilty for not telling her what I know about her brother, but I bombarded her with enough information today.

"Tristan?" Katherine says, breaking the uncomfortable silence. I murmur a "huh" in my throat, and she continues after a moment. "You already knew my story when you met me. Why did you have me tell it?"

This is an easy one to answer. Once the questions get more detailed is when I'll really squirm. She can't know I'm in love with her; not yet. She would think I'm crazy, just chasing after a girl I've never actually met for two years, and expecting her to fall in love with me instantly. She doesn't know of all the letters we've shared, although I didn't know it was her I was writing to until she told me about David.

No, I will not confess my love for her so soon, with such a heavy secret on my shoulders.

"I wanted to hear it from you. I wanted confirmation that you trust me," I answer simply, digging my feet into the horses' sides, making Dino trot faster. "I didn't want to push you into telling me, but at the same time, I wanted to hear you say it aloud, just to confirm what I already knew. Sometimes it's nice hearing things out loud," I finish, feeling foolish and immature.

To my surprise and delight, Katherine leans back into my chest, placing a quick kiss on my cheek before settling her head on my shoulder. I smile, thankful she can't see my face, which undoubtedly has the goofiest grin imaginable plastered on it. I try to slow my breathing, which has quickened due to Katie's proximity and the thrill of riding again, in an attempt to jostle her head as little as possible. It isn't working, and my breaths come in hard gasps. It'll be a miracle if she doesn't move away from me.

She doesn't. In fact, we stay this way the entire ride home, which is faster than before thanks to Dino's quickened pace. We arrive at the barn just as the sun begins to disappear behind the hill, and I'm sad to have to leave Katherine after being so close to her all day. Her light has filled me, leaving a pleasant feeling of warmth in its wake. Shutting Dino into his stall, I walk across the barn and find Katherine sitting on the couch, eyes closed, lips whispering silent words into the empty air.

"All set," I say, making her jump. Laughing, I apologize.

"I'd invite you to stay for dinner, but I'm not positive my aunt wouldn't hit on you," she says, eyes widening slightly when she finished talking, cheeks reddening an adorable shade of rose.

Catching her eye, I raise my eyebrows and smirk. "You think I'm attractive?" I tease, lightly bumping my shoulder against hers. She watches her feet as we walk, but I can see her cheeks flush even more.

Suddenly, she looks up at me, the setting sun leaving a glint of light in her big green eyes. "How do you know my aunt? I know it's a small town, but you seemed awfully... comfortable with her horse today. Unless you're just a horse whisperer," she jokes, but the curiosity is practically dripping from her words.

I groan internally, not wanting to further elaborate on my story at the moment. "Why don't we save the questions for another day, and just enjoy the walk," I say, releasing her hand and slyly putting my arm around her tiny shoulders. I feel her relax, which makes me relax.

"Promise?" she says, looking up at me through thick, dark eyelashes. Every time she blinks, my heart flutters a little faster; she bats her eyes instead of blinks. I try to think about manly things, like football and cars, but I'm too content to pretend to be something I'm not. I just let the flutters fill me and revel in her presence.

"I promise," I chuckle, feeling her arm wrap around my waist. I feel something seep into me; something I've never felt before. It's a warmth, a sugary sweetness that makes my mouth water. *"What's up with this?"* I think to myself, and just as I think the words, I know the answer.

It's happiness; Katherine's happiness.

Chapter 8

Katherine

Tristan walks up the front stairs with me, arm releasing my shoulders and hand grasping mine. Bringing it to his lips, he kisses it before stepping back onto the front lawn. I open the unlocked door, not taking my eyes off his.

"Thanks for… the fun ride," I say lamely, unable to come up with something more creative. "Fun" was an understatement…

He smirks, shoving his hands into the pockets of his jeans. "Anytime, Katie. I'll see you tomorrow. Do you want a ride to school?" he asks, shifting his weight from one foot to the other.

Stomach teeming with butterflies, I have to physically force myself to not jump up and down. Crossing my ankles, I lean against the doorframe. "Sure," is all I can say without squealing like a five year old.

Tristan nods, winking a blue eye at me. "Pick you up at quarter after seven, ok?" I nod, letting my smile widen. "Well, until then, sweet dreams, Katherine," he says, and then he turns on his heel and walks off towards the road. I didn't realize he hadn't brought a car here.

Spinning around in the doorway, I walk inside and shut the door just as the last ray of sun disappears from the sky, following Tristan down the road. I place a hand over my mouth, feeling my quickened breaths beat against my palm.

I'm emotionally exhausted, but the idea of closing my eyes seems crazy. There is too much to process that I haven't even begun to think about. The fact that everything is falling into place so perfectly doesn't seem real. My life isn't like this; fairytales don't happen to sinners like me. They happen to the pretty cheerleaders who are Mother Teresa's great-great-granddaughters who haven't been deemed mentally unstable.

Yet it is happening; my fairytale is coming true. Tristan is so much more than what he seems, and he seemed pretty great before I even really knew him. The fact that he and I were interconnected so deeply that God himself fashioned our souls into one entity was unfathomable. A happiness and peace soars so high in my heart that I feel like I will float away if a good wind sweeps in. I haven't felt happiness like this in all my life, never before have I felt so light.

It's as though my world has stopped its orbit in the solar system, bypassing the sun and every other planet in its path, making its way to its true destination. My world revolves around a new sun, a sun sent to me from the Lord himself to coat my world, not in darkness, but in light.

The tall, wooden grandfather clock in the dining room chimes seven times. I didn't realize how much time Tristan and I spent on the hill today, but now that my mind is beginning to comprehend the situation, my human body begins to fail me once again. A wave of exhaustion rolls over me just as headlights streak through the window, painting the interior walls with artificial brightness. I squint before running down the hall and into the bathroom.

Not in the mood to talk any more, I rush to jump in the shower so Aunt Rachel can't badger me with questions about my day. I wasn't going to tell anybody about it, so she could just keep her questions to herself.

I stop scrubbing my hair, stunned with a sudden revelation. All day, I hadn't felt anything out of place. Anything meaning… feelings. I felt nothing I wasn't supposed to; no guilt, no jealousy, no overwhelming sadness. Nothing but pure contentment. My eyes widen slightly and I wonder why my punishment was revoked for the day. Usually, an errant thought would send me into a tizzy of knots and give me a stomach ache that would make the world go fuzzy.

It's Tristan, I think. When he and I are together, our punishments balance the others; he feels my every feeling, but can make them go away by simply touching my hand. When he takes it away I'm free to feel happiness again, and that feeling seeps into him. That explains why he was so eager to touch me; he wanted to make himself feel better. Sure, I bet he wanted to make me more comfortable too, but now that I had a reason to doubt his kindness, I felt the familiar pangs of greed and sadness.

Greed is a funny thing; it tastes like a penny, if you were to lick it. It isn't just a word to describe a self-centered person, either... No, it was a word to describe a person who wanted what they didn't or couldn't have. I wanted Tristan; I knew he was rightfully mine, in some way, but that didn't mean I could just swoop in and take him.

A peculiar sensation washes through me, running over my skin like the hot water of my shower. It feels almost like... foam. I feel the need to close my eyes, and once I do, I see three words sprawled across my closed eyelids.

Love,

Betrayal,

Peace.

Call it intuition, inspiration, or wishful thinking, but I know these words will be somehow connected with Tristan. It makes sense; he floated into my life like a dandelion seed, planting rays of hope and promises of new beginnings. Two out of the three words I just saw made sense, but what was betrayal doing in there? Like a black sheep in a Shepard's herd, it stood out to me the most, leaving a feeling of dread behind.

A fist pounding on the door jars my attention back to where I am and what I'm doing; aimlessly standing in the shower, daydreaming. Briefly, a flashback plays across my vision, and I can see my father's fist pounding against the wall.

"Katherine, what in the hell are you doing in there? I got home an hour ago, girl! Come on out so we can chat," Aunt Rachel yells so I could hear her over the roar of the running water.

"Okay!" I shout back, surprising myself. I'm not one to give unnecessary replies, and I could feel a smile creeping up on my face as I turned off the water and began to towel dry my curly locks.

Yes, things were changing. Quicker than I would've thought possible, I could feel the broken heart in my chest begin to mend.

* * *

Standing in front of my pathetic excuse for a closet, I wrack my brains for any reason as to why my uniform skirt would not be on its proper hanger. No, I'm not an obsessive-compulsive person, but if my skirt was missing, I would be forced to wear the horrible black dress-slacks as a Plan-B.

Aunt Rachel had gone to the barn about an hour ago to take care of the horses and I still haven't told her of my day with Tristan. She had been to the barn last night and commented on the saddle being moved, but I simply shrugged it off and continued to eat. Knowing that she somehow knew Tristan bothered me, but simply because I hated unsolved mysteries.

Taking one final glance in my closet, I see the skirt buried beneath a sweatshirt, wrinkled and unwashed. I cuss under my breath, resigning myself to wearing those awful dress-pants. At seven fifteen, I run a brush through my hair, which is wavier than curly today. My green eyes stand out the most on my plain face, which is quite unremarkable if you ask me. I sigh, wondering what made me special enough to warrant a visit from God. Wondering what made me special enough to deserve a second chance… to deserve Tristan.

Three knocks signaled on the front door, making me run down the hall, feet barely touching the floor. I force myself to take a deep breath before opening the door, but I can't wait another second to see his face.

I am not disappointed. His light blonde hair seems to be growing precariously longer as the day's pass; I usually notice little details like this about people. Blue eyes sparkling, wearing his worn leather jacket over his school uniform, he looks like a dark, dangerous angel as the sun casts its rays upon his handsome face. Butterflies form in my stomach as I realize that he is, truly, an angel in a bad boy disguise.

"Good morning," he drawls, breaking my stare with his charming smile.

"Hi," I say lamely, a blush creeping up on my cheeks. "Um, let me grab my backpack and then we can go."

Tristan nods and I run across the room to get my bag, turning on my heel and walking back to the door. He hasn't moved from his spot on the porch, and as we descend the stairs he holds his hand out to me. His beautiful face is silhouetted against the sun, making his strong, square jaw look even more appealing. Instead of taking his hand, I find myself cocking my head and simply staring at him.

He laughs nervously, obviously confused at my current fixation. Unable to avert my eyes, I hear God's words ring through my head once more; "*Keep your eyes open, Katherine, because he is not an angel in your sense of the word.*"

"Tristan, there's something you're not telling me," I say as he opens the passenger door to his black Chevy. He offers me his hand again and this time I take it, but realize it's just there to help me climb into the tall, rusty truck.

I watch as he walks leisurely around the front of the vehicle and climbs into the drivers' side and starts the engine. We make it halfway down my long driveway before he speaks again.

"And what makes you think that?" he says, patiently, but not denying my statement.

"Besides the fact that you told me?" I say, and he smirks, casting a sarcastic glance at me. "I was told my angel wouldn't look like an angel; that I wouldn't expect him to be who I was looking for," I say, trailing off, unable to form coherent thoughts with his smile momentarily dazing me.

"Thanks, I'll take that as a compliment," Tristan jokes, "But maybe He didn't mean physically, Katie. To anybody else, I'm no angel."

"You're mine," I say, interrupting him without thinking. I just couldn't stop myself; if he was an angel for anybody else, I would go insane with jealousy.

He chuckles and leans over to plant a quick, sweet kiss on my cheek, making my heart beat furiously and cheeks burn bright with satisfaction.

"That I am. Thank you for that," he says, holding my hand on his lap. "But what I meant was, to everyone else, I'm bad news. I'm glad you got to see me before you heard everyone else's opinions; that's a blessing in itself."

I squeeze his hand. No one has said anything to me about Tristan, but mostly more than half the school left the day I arrived here. Gone for the past two weeks on a class trip to Germany, I was left with only a few peers who were either deadbeats who didn't even try conversing with me, or on academic suspension and we're allowed on the trip. I hadn't felt the need to make friends with those left behind. Scott and the girls who originally tormented Tristan in the garden were touring the streets of Berlin, out of sight and out of mind. That is, until today.

We pull into the student parking lot to find it jam packed with fancy looking cars; all colors, all makes and models, but most of them very swanky looking. I thought I heard Tristan cuss under his breath, but he remained as stoic as ever.

"Looks like the trip is over," I say, looking out the windows at the swarm of people milling about, all dressed in similar shades of gray and maroon.

Tristan just looks straight ahead, the corner of his mouth twitching. He pulls into the parking space closest to the door, and I'm surprised it's not taken already.

"No matter what you hear, please don't listen," he says, voice so desperate I'm forced to look at him. His blue eyes are pained, but his face doesn't hint at any emotion at all. Again, I feel a brief moment of happiness that I don't need to feel such obtrusive things when I'm with him.

I touch his tanned cheek with my free hand, feeling his smooth, unblemished skin under my fingertips. He visibly relaxes; his shoulders slump forward and upper-back releases its tension.

He turns his face and kisses my palm, sending an embarrassing shiver through my body.

"I won't have a chance to listen if I'm with you all day," I say, winking, reaching for my backpack at my feet. I catch Tristan smiling to himself with a faint flush on his cheeks, which is so adorable I release a giggle.

"I think I could deal with that. Don't even think about opening that door," he says, pointing to my hand on the door handle.

I give him a confused look, to which he just laughs. In the next moment, he's opening it for me and helping me down. I look up at him through my eyelashes, weakly making an attempt at looking flirtatious, which is pathetic. Instead of laughing at my stupidity, he smirks, causing my stomach to flip.

"Do you need to stop at your locker?" Tristan asks, tucking a stray hair of mine behind my ear, making me shiver.

I shake my head and start walking towards the school, grabbing his hand and pulling him along with me. I double take at the massive crowd of people openly gawking at us. The girls all seem to have their eyebrows raised with shocked expressions and the guys seem genuinely freaked out. Instead of acknowledging the others, Tristan pulls me closer to his side and picks up our pace.

Confused, I pull Tristan into a nook at the end of the hallway, seeking shelter from the watchful eyes that followed us as we entered the school. "Tristan, what was that?" I say, shocked and, to be honest, kind of pissed off.

He leans against the window, running his hands over his face, shaking his head slightly. "They know... what happened to me. I kind of... lost it, for a while..." he struggles to continue, due to embarrassment, anger, frustration, or a combination of the three, I don't know.

I boldly wrap an arm around his waist, pulling myself closer to him; so close that I can see a tiny scar just over his lip, one I hadn't seen before. Instinctively, I want to touch it, and I need to literally force my hand to stay at my side. "They know," I state, understanding.

They know Tristan blanked out after his sister's death, but what they don't know is the fact that he is trying his damn hardest to make things right again. He isn't a boy flooded with guilt; all he is now is a young man in the process of getting his life back together.

"Let them think what they want to think," I say, hugging him tighter for a moment before stepping back and grabbing his hand again. "Come on, the warning bell just rang."

We walk into AP Government together, feeling fifteen pairs of eyes boring into our skin. Fingers still locked, we scan the room for seats next to each other and miraculously find some directly in front of the room. Tristan pulls us over towards them as the final bell rings, no one breaking the awkward silence that filled the room as soon as we walked in.

If you asked me what we learned in class that day, I would've told you the one thing I learned; Tristan is a genius. He scribbled notes furiously as Mrs. Hollis continued on with her lesson. I watched out of the corner of my eye as he kept his right hand locked with mine; thank God he is left handed, because I never want to let go of him.

When the bell rings, signaling that first period is over, I jump, having been daydreaming deeply. Glancing automatically at Tristan, I see that he is already standing, my book-bag and his slung over his broad shoulders.

"English," he says, smiling. I nod, standing tentatively on my legs, afraid they would crumple under me.

We make our way through the crowded hallway, Tristan inadvertently making an easy path for us to go through. I keep my eyes trained on his back, willing myself not to look at the judging faces observing us. Free period passes, and soon we are on our way to English.

"Crap," I mutter, walking into the room beside him. Tristan quirks a brow at me and I explain that I need to go to my locker and get my notebook. He takes a seat, setting my bag onto the desk beside him. Not like anyone would take it anyways with the looks he's been given this morning.

At my locker, I hear the final bell ring, but take my time. Mr. Morrison gave me permission to leave the room, so I'm not in need of a pass. I hear the clicking of heels behind me and turn to see the dark skinned girl I hadn't seen since my first day. She smiled warmly at me, but it looked plastic. Just like she did.

"Hi," she says in a singsong voice, dripping with false charm. "You're Katherine Prince. I haven't formally introduced myself to you. I'm Malaya Garzon, maybe you've heard of me?"

I shove down the urge to burst out laughing. This girl was the typical cheerleader stereotype, which I can recognize from a mile away. Remembering her cruel words directed towards Tristan and I, I merely smile, not saying anything, and turn to shut my locker.

"So, you're Tristan's new play toy?" she says, eyes cutting.

Forcing my expression to remain calm, I feign a look of confused innocence. "Play toy? I don't think that's the proper title; girlfriend is more appropriate." *Soul mate is more appropriate, actually,* I add silently.

Malaya just laughs a shrill and demeaning sound that sends prickles to the surface of my skin. I can feel frustration and hostility rolling off her, and I'm disappointed my old "knack" for detecting emotions is making a reappearance.

"Honestly honey, there's not a girl at this school that hasn't been with Tristan Parker Presidio. I'm just warning you, the guy's a psycho. His like, whole family was killed in some awful fire or accident or something like that, and Tristan totally went off the deep end; drugs, gangs, drinking, carjacking, you name it!" she says, voice laced with contempt and I can tell she's just itching to share this gossip with new ears.

I am not a violent person; on the contrary, I am extremely non-confrontational. In this moment, I feel the burning desire to slap Malaya across the face simply because she's speaking ill of Tristan. Instead of being rash and acting out my physical frustrations on this dimwitted girl, I slap her with the most powerful thing in my arsenal; words.

"Listen, Malaya," I sneer her name. "For future reference, get your facts straight when you're telling someone else's story. I'm not interested in any information you have to give me, so please get out of my way," I say, voice deadly quiet.

She stands there, mouth slightly open, eyes filled with shock and pure rage. "I'm just trying to help you out, Katherine," she says, faking hurt. I can feel what she's really feeling, which is anger and jealousy. Mhm… that's interesting.

"I don't need any help, but thanks anyways," I say, voice dripping with a sarcastic venom I didn't knew existed in me. Silently, I say a prayer apologizing for my behavior just now, but I'm still too frustrated to be completely heartfelt.

Opening the door to English, I keep my eyes averted from those staring at me as I take my seat. Mr. Morrison continues his lecture on the personalities of Elizabeth Bennett and Mr. Darcy, and I feel Tristan's finger tracing a circle on my clenched fist resting on my desk. Relaxing at the contact, I lose myself in the words spewing from our teachers' mouth.

During our second free period it beings to rain outside, so we forgo our bench in the garden for a table in the library.

"What do you think about Mr. Darcy?" Tristan asks, distracting me from my AP Calc homework.

I look up, pleased to have an excuse to ignore my very difficult homework. "I think he's fantastic," I say with a genuine smile.

His eyebrows shoot up, a look of pure disbelief coating his angelic face. "How so? He's such an asshole to Lizzie and he's insanely arrogant. What about that is appealing to you?" Tristan asks, leaning towards me over the tiny library table.

"He's just trying to do what's best for her! So what if he's got some major ego problems? He's the picture of gentlemanly swag," I joke, wondering if all boys have the same opinions of Mr. Darcy as Tristan does. In fact, I wonder if any other boys in our class are actually reading the book.

"How is being stuck up and narcissistic attractive? He hurt her while 'trying to do what's best for her,'" he quotes with his fingers.

"At least he tried to help out! He believed Mr. Bingley was going to get heartbroken by Jane, so he intervened. Yeah, it was a stupid move from Lizzie's point of view, but that's because she didn't see his reasoning behind it. Darcy was only doing what he thought was best for his friend, so that makes him honorable and forgivable, don't you think?" I challenge.

Tristan purses his lips and shakes his head, inciting a laugh from me. "The guy's an idiot; he almost lost Lizzie because of his stupid Aunt and his own ego. Could you ever imagine one of your family members taking away the love of your life?" he asks rhetorically.

"His aunt never took Lizzie away; she just threatened their relationship," I correct, unable to let him butcher such a key point in the plot line of my favorite novel.

"You get my point," he drawls, leaning back in his chair, hands locked behind his neck. "I'd kill myself if that ever happened."

Our eyes lock as we realize the ironic seriousness of what he just said. A moment of awkward silence passes, but Tristan leans forward again, reaching towards me and taking my hands in his.

"I need to learn to watch my words," he says, a small smile gracing his features. "Katie, calm down, please."

I grip his hands and stare into his blue eyes, which look gray in the dim light of the library. In that moment, I want nothing more than to kiss him; to feel his lips on mine.

"Why haven't you kissed me?" I blurt out, mouth acting of its own accord and forming the words that bubbled in my throat. "I'm sorry, I didn't mean to say that aloud," I say, embarrassed.

To my surprise, Tristan takes on a look of surprise. "Can you read minds, too? I was just about to ask you the same question," he says, leaning on his elbows.

My eyebrows gather in the middle, furrowing. "You're the boy; you make the first move. It's traditional," I offer, as if it's common sense, which I thought it was.

Maybe he just doesn't want to kiss me. Maybe he thinks we're moving too fast and he's getting freaked out by how heavy and serious our "relationship" is getting so soon. But we're supposed to do this with each other. We were made to be a whole; to help one another find themself again. This- being together- feels as natural as breathing, and I thought he felt it too. Shame and embarrassment floods through me at the thought that he doesn't want me the way I want him.

Again, his eyebrows shoot up, a look of panic in his eyes, and I realize I had forgotten that he can feel what I feel upon contact.

"Katherine! You're ridiculous," he says, pulling his hands from mine and standing from his chair. For a moment, I'm terrified he's going to hit me, or walk away and never come back, which makes me think of my father, which makes me want to cry.

"Katie," he says, kneeling down next to my chair, hands resting on my knees.

I close my eyes, choking on the feelings welling up inside of me. I haven't missed this feeling of powerlessness, and I wish my Punishment would go away permanently. Tristan takes my hands, bringing them to his face.

"Sweetheart, we're in this together," he whispers, eyes closing. I can almost see the transfer of energy as my sadness, fear, shame, and embarrassment float from my heart to his as he takes away my painful feelings.

We sit there for what feels like hours, eyes closed and feeling completely content just to be next to the other. The warning bell rings, signaling our return to reality.

"I don't care that it's a Monday," Tristan says as we walk to his truck at the end of the day. "I'm taking you out tonight, if you'll have me Juliet," he teases.

I groan. "Please, no Romeo and Juliet references! The last thing we need is to end up like them," I say, shuddering at the thought.

He chuckles, tucking me under his arm as the misty rain coats our clothing in its feathery lightness "Touché, but we have something they didn't," he says ominously.

I quirk my head to the side, urging him on. "Fate himself designed our future; He wouldn't approve of a tragic ending when He went through so much trouble to make things right for us, right?" he winks, so carefree.

Smiling, I lean into him, enveloped in the scent of Tristan, which is a woodsy, cinnamon, light cologne type of smell that makes my stomach flutter. I really hope we have a better chance than Romeo and Juliet; Tristan is right, though. We have God on our side.

Chapter 9

Tristan takes me home right after school, but I don't want our time together to end. I feel like a drug addict, hooked on the boy beside me.

"Could you stay for a while? I could really use your expertise with my AP Calc," I ask, flirtingly batting my eyes and smiling, trying to lift my heavy spirit.

"You're great at math, who are you kidding?" he shoots back as he kills the engine, parking his truck in my driveway. "But I'll stay," he winks, flirting back.

Hopping out of the car, I see Aunt Rachel walk around the side of the house, eyebrows raised up to the brim of her large gardening hat. Her car isn't here, so I assumed she was working, like she usually is.

"A-Aunt Rachel-l," I stutter, flustered by the expression on her face.

"Katherine, I didn't know you knew Tristan," she says, a smile forming on her lips. "Why haven't you told me you made friends, Trist?" Aunt Rachel says, walking towards him with arms wide open.

He seems a little surprised, but walks into her embrace, hugging her back. I'm sure my face portrayed my shock, but I was more frustrated than anything else; how well did these two know each other, and why hadn't Tristan told me everything? Why hadn't Rachel?

"I figured the gossip would get to you eventually," he laughs, releasing her.

"It's not as good as seeing the real thing with my own two eyes, now is it?" Aunt Rachel says, smoothing down Tristan's hair, which is spiking up in the front.

Tristan seems to be avoiding my stare, but there's no doubt he senses my aggravation.

"Where's your car, Aunt Rachel? And why aren't you at work?" I ask, crossing my arms, which makes my shirt sleeves ride up. I'm still uncomfortable having my scars out in the open, but the breeze feels nice.

"Broke down on the highway before I got three miles from home," she says, taking off her hat and batting away non-existent dirt. "Called the taxi and came straight home. Figured I could go a day without being in the office, especially a day as fine as today," Aunt Rachel finishes, gesturing to the now clear sky with her hands.

I don't believe her for a second. There is something too innocent about her expression, and it makes me uneasy. Instead of pressing when it's obvious she wants to avoid details, I just nod my head but send her a look that says "we'll talk about this later."

"Why don't you take her to the barn, Tristan? I'm sure she'd love a ride," Aunt Rachel says, wiping the sweat off her forehead. It had gotten very humid, which supports my conclusion that Montana weather is bipolar.

Tristan goes to say something, but I cut him off, not wanting Aunt Rachel to know we have already been to the barn. "As much as I'd like to ride with Tristan, I think we're gonna do some homework," I say, then blush furiously when I hear the double-meaning bchind my words.

Aunt Rachel starts laughing, a cackling sound that makes me blush even more. "Well honey, I won't have to worry about you gettin' steamy with Tristan here if you've got some homework to do instead of havin' a bit of fun," she says, laughing so hard tears stream down her youthful face. I don't know why she finds the situation so humorous, but it's ticking me off.

"Alright, going inside now!" I say, attempting to avoid any more discomfort.

"Tristan, you're stayin' for dinner now, you hear?" Rachel calls to us as we walk up the stairs, backpacks in hand.

He nods, looking peaceful. Once I open the door, he hesitates before stepping over the threshold. I motion with my head for him to come in, and once he does, I shut the door behind him.

"You've got some explaining to do," I wag my finger back and forth, teasing and serious at the same time.

It's like he didn't even hear me; his eyes roam the room and his expression turns ice cold. Without warning, he bends down and rips his boots off before walking down the hallway and out of sight. I follow after him, eyebrow cocked, pausing to set my bag on the ground in the dining room.

"Tristan?" I say, confused and worried. This is strange.

I walk down the hall slowly, peering into each room to see where he is. Is this some type of game? When I get to my bedroom, door ajar and Tristan staring at the wall, I'm about to explode with frustrated confusion.

"This is your room?" he asks, voice cracking slightly.

"Yeah," I say, not sure how else to fill the silence.

"Your favorite color is blue, isn't it?"

I walk until I'm standing next to him, our arms touching. "Yes, it is. What's going...?" I was about to say, "What's going through that head of yours," but he silences me by pulling me under his arm. His comforting gesture would be nothing more than that- a comforting gesture- if not for the trembling of his hands and tensed muscles.

"Let's go for a walk," he whispers into my hair, so lightly I can barely hear him. His deep voice sounds extra sultry in this moment, and the corners of my mouth turn up despite my frustration.

I nod, and then take his hand, expecting to lead him out, but he pulls me along instead.

"Be right back, Rachel! Going for a walk," he yells out the kitchen window to my gardening aunt.

We don't wait to hear her response, just walk out the front door, barely closing it behind me before Tristan leaps down the steps in haste.

"You need to promise me something else," Tristan says, eyes empty, face guarded.

"Anything," I respond, pulling his hand to my mouth, kissing his knuckles. This gesture surprises me; I never initiate physical affection.

He watches me for a moment, studying my face and hands. "That you'll trust me no matter what," he says, but the words hitch at the end, making the sentence sound like a question.

"I trust you, no matter what. I promise," I say, begging, desperate to know more; to solve the mystery that is Tristan Presidio.

He moves in front of me, walking backwards while keeping one hand in mine. "Then close your eyes," he says, free hand lifts to my face, covering my eyes, which close immediately.

"Is this some super-secret-spot that nobody knows about?" I say, attempting to lighten the mood.

"No," he says, voice still serious and sexy. "I just like having proof that you trust me."

His words make me sad and I can't keep the frown off my face. About what I judge to be ten minutes later, he gently pulls me to a stop. "Open your eyes, Katie," he says, running his big hand through my hair.

The beauty of the landscape will never cease to amaze me; the rolling hills and massive snowcapped mountains in the distance are like Disneyland to a child for the first time, wondrous and vast. Breathtaking.

Before I can speak, he guides me towards a boulder resting on the edge of the cliff-like structure we're standing on, which is looking out over the land. Scooting over to make room for me, he pats the spot beside him, gesturing for me to sit down. I surprise myself yet again by denying his offer and walking to the front of the rock before sliding on, seated between his now open legs. He pulls me close, lining up our bodies, which mold perfectly with one another. My impatience returns, leaving a bitter taste on my tongue. Figuratively, for once.

"Come on, Tristan. It's time for some answers," I say, breaking the peace around us with my voice.

I feel his arms wrap around me a little tighter, and instinctively tilt my head back to see his face better. Instead of finding comfort in his blue eyes, I see the tenseness of his square jaw, smarting with pressure as he clenches his teeth.

"I've known Rachel for a while, Katie. Wh-when I, um… sh-she," he stammers. This is the first time I've ever heard Tristan so unsure of himself; he has a graceful flow to his speech most of the time.

I wait patiently for him to continue, urging him on with my silence. "My mom kicked me out of the house the first time I was arrested," he says.

"Arrested? What were you arrested for?" I ask, trying to stay calm, but my voice raises a few octaves.

"I got caught downtown with some guys I thought were my friends. They planted three bags of weed on me when the cops showed up, and some speed was stuffed in my pocket," he says, sounding guilty and ashamed.

I squeeze his knee in reassurance, but only because I'm too stunned to speak.

"So anyway, my mom wanted to put me in temporary foster care. The court wouldn't give the go-ahead, so she took action herself and Rachel was the first volunteer. For five months, she homeschooled me, I lived in her house, slept in what is now your bedroom, ate in her kitchen… basically, it was stay-at-home therapy," he continues, voice growing somewhat bitter.

"How come you never told me this? Did you think this wasn't worth sharing with me?" I ask, pulling away from him to see his face. The shock there was obvious, but the sting in my chest didn't recede; I'm upset he wasn't completely honest with me, even after I told him everything. I feel anger working its way through my veins, and I attempt to control my blood from boiling.

"Katherine, I just don't want to scare you off!" he says, pushing a piece of hair behind my ear. "It isn't easy to retell this sort of stuff, alright? It isn't like this is some funny old story!" he says, voice fierce and eyes shining, tinted with something that looks an awful lot like anger.

I scoff, frustrated. "Tristan, you think you can scare me off? Don't you think if I was going to run, I would have by now?" I stand, trying to stop the heat of my intensified anger from spewing foul words from my mouth. "I'm the person you're supposed to trust!"

The flash of heat in my veins is unnatural, meaning the effects of my Punishment are seeping into my blood. I watch as Tristan runs a hand over his face, a gesture saved for when he is under stress. My brother used to do the same thing, and I feel a twinge of sorrow at the fact that he hasn't contacted me in weeks.

"Do you just want me to say it? Flat-out tell you what I've been keeping from you?" asks Tristan, sounding nervous but just as frustrated as I feel, but I don't know why he would be irritated. I'm not the one keeping secrets.

"Yes!" I answer, lifting my hands up in a way that says "are you stupid?"

"Fine," he says, standing from the boulder and stepping towards me. "I stayed with Rachel before going to the same boarding school your brother went to. He was in my therapy group, and he talked an awful lot about *you*."

My mouth pops open, but no words crawl up my throat. He knew David? He was friends with David? "You were friends with my brother?" I ask quietly.

He shakes his head, rocking back on his heels slightly. "No, Katherine. Dave wasn't exactly friend material," his eyes take on a sympathetic look.

"What do you mean?" I ask, confused.

Tristan sighs, long and deep and full of something I can't decipher. "Katie, I wrote those letters to you. The ones you thought David sent you? That was me," he says, not meeting my gaze. "Your brother isn't... stable. He was transferred to a mental facility in California where he still is... until further notice."

My stomach drops. That's why "David" hasn't returned my last letter, because Tristan was probably at Rachel's by then. I haven't talked to my brother in months, but I assumed my parents have kept in touch with him and his advisors

My brother was diagnosed with a split-personality disorder that turned him from a loving, quiet, gentle boy into a screaming, homicidal madman. I had only ever seen one of his episodes, but it was scary as hell, not to mention extremely unpredictable. Pushing the flashbacks out of my mind, containing them inside the glass bubble that I've protected myself with all these years, I lash out instead of coping with the pain.

"Why would you write letters to me? How did the facility let you do that?! You were letting me believe he was getting better! That he loved me and would come see me soon and that he was living his life carefree and..." I get cut off by the sob that escaped me, and I couldn't stop the tears that followed. I feel angry, but also betrayed, and my mind flashes to the words that popped into my head while I was showering. Maybe this is the betrayal I was warned about.

Oddly enough, I'm not sure it's Tristan I'm angry at: Maybe it's the world, for being so unpredictable and unkind to those of us trying to get by. Maybe I'm just angry at myself for not being the sister David needed and contacting him more often. The doctors had told us he wasn't in any condition to speak with us, so I could never call. A break with reality, that's what they called it. My anger, no matter who it's directed towards, sends the tears down my cheeks in a cascading river of confusion and sorrow.

"Katherine, please don't be upset," Tristan begged, frantically wiping the tears from my face. In this moment, I don't want him to touch me, to take away my pain. I'm not the fragile, weepy girl that Tristan sees me as; I've let happiness soften me, and I don't like feeling vulnerable.

I pull away from him, not out of anger, but out of necessity. I cannot think straight when he touches me. David was never a permanent fixture in my life, but rather a memory that has faded with the passage of time. His letters made him seem real again, and now that I know that my brother was never really talking to me, telling me things that made me laugh and hope, I feel hollow.

Deep down, I always thought his letters were too good to be true. In the months following his initial check-in, David wrote me no letters at all. I can see where his path probably intersected with Tristan's, but their relationship is still confusing.

"Why would you write letters to me? You didn't even know me!" I say, wiping my face off and desperately wishing I had a tissue.

"When I stayed with Rachel, a few months after…" he trails off, looking down, and I realize that he's uncomfortable speaking about his attempted suicide.

I can say words like "suicide" without cringing, because words are nothing more than letters. They are describers of actions, and these actions are what support our futures. It's not words I fear, but what they stand for.

Tristan continues. "I felt like I was doing so well with the help of Rachel. She was so kind to me, and I was a new person within a matter of weeks. The only reason I was even sent to John Adam's was because Rachel said it would look better, that people would believe *I* was better, if I went to a facility. Not only that, but Adam's offers high school classes and I was so behind I would've had to be held back. She sent me there because David was there, and she felt like I could… somehow connect with him because we shared her acquaintance in common.

"Once I got there, I immediately knew there would be no getting through to your brother. He…"

"What, Tristan? He what?" I say, anxiously awaiting him to continue.

He sighs, licking his bottom lip, making it shiny and tempting. "He wouldn't even speak, Katie. We would be forcefully taken from his room to the dining hall, and I felt sorry for Rachel. I snuck into his room the first week I got there, and found a stack of unopened letters on his desk. I took the letters, left the room, and read them all."

Tristan really does know me; everything about me. When I was experiencing a particularly difficult thing, I would pour my heart out in those letters I sent to David. Even if he wasn't answering, I wrote to him. Tristan knows about the abuse from my father, my mother's drinking problem, petty arguments with old friends... everything.

"Why? Did you even know I was Rachel's niece?" I ask, trying to get as much information as possible.

"Yeah, I knew you were her niece," his eyes take on a look of longing, and of sensitivity I have never seen in anyone's. "Katie, you sent David a picture of you and him. Remember? That photo of the two of you on the steps?"

I nod; it's the same photo I keep in my wallet. Tristan reaches into his back pocket, hand emerging a second later holding a folded piece of paper. He opens it, folds it over again so that the photograph is facing the outside, and hands it to me. Sure enough, it's the photograph I sent David, upon his request.

"I don't believe in coincidences, Katie. When I saw your signature at the end of each letter, saw your name, I couldn't help but ask you to send me a picture of yourself, to validate what I suspected. It was you, the girl from my vision, the angel God told me he sent," Tristan smiles, a weak one compared with others I've seen.

"And you couldn't tell me because... I would never have believed you," I whisper, still shocked.

"And because I just couldn't bear to tell you about David... I thought that would be the final straw; that you would just give up," he says, and I realize he fully believes he was doing the right thing.

"So you knew who I was all along. You knew I was Rachel's niece, so why did you act so unknowing the first few days after we met?"

"Katie, I want everything to work out for us. I didn't know how to explain all this to you without making you upset. And obviously, I haven't done a good job, anyways," he says, face taking on an apologetic grimace as he strokes my hair.

"So, David never talked?" I ask, sniffing.

"Yeah, he did, just... selectively. He didn't like me very much; he thought I was some type of dangerous stalker because I tried getting him to talk about you. David was volatile, to say the least," Tristan says, smiling. "He only ever said the same thing, though. 'I want sissy happy.'"

I smile, thinking of the David that taught me to ride a bike and had lemonade stands with me when we were children. That David is merely a memory now, if what Tristan says is true. And since I have no reason to doubt him, I believe him.

"So, when did you come home?" I ask, wanting to stray from talk of my brother for a few minutes.

"About a week before the first day of school. The last letter I got from you was sent from the hospital you were in, days after you tried to…" he struggles, but I nod so he knows I know what he's talking about. "You said you were going to stay with Rachel, and you left an address. I called Rachel, who called my advisor, who let me come home."

"Where is 'home' for you? I meant to ask earlier. I got the impression your mother was a… uh…" I trail off, unsure what to say to fill in the blank.

"Bitch?" he says, eyes hardening. "She changed after my dad died. A lot. But yeah, she and I aren't on speaking terms. Rachel helped me get my own apartment, in her name, and I live there. It isn't bad for a guy who's barely eighteen. Granted I haven't been able to do much with it just yet, but it'll be great soon enough."

I understand why Aunt Rachel wouldn't have told me about Tristan; his past is too frightening to share with a niece she's just getting to know. The fact that my aunt cares enough about Tristan to keep his past, and present, a secret shows mounds about her character.

A few minutes pass and I just sit, thinking but not thinking. More like soaking, absorbing the information like a sponge. Tristan sits on the grass in front of where I'm sitting, and a slight breeze pushes strands of his hair into his blue eyes, which are assessing mine. I reach up and push the strands back, not wanting to have it as a barrier between us.

"I should get you back. We have dinner to eat, you know. I promised I'd stay," Tristan says, voice quiet and sultry.

I nod, but make no move to stand. Tristan stands, towering over me, holding out both of his hands to help me up. I just stare at them, wondering when he's going to poof into a cloud, proving he's a figment of my imagination. I don't know what's real anymore.

Settling on reality, I grab his hands and stand, but he surprises me yet again by gently guiding me into a hug. Enveloped in his tanned arms, I inhale the strong, masculine scent that no cologne maker could ever perfect. We just stand there, his arms around my waist, mine around his neck. His build is athletic, strong and muscled, but somehow tall and lean. How I ever thought of him as frightening is beyond me, because I have never felt safer than I do in this moment.

* * *

When we arrive back at the house, Aunt Rachel is in the kitchen, bumping pots and pans into countertops and stumbling on her own two feet. The sight brings a smile to my face and Tristan's light kiss on my cheek makes me shine even brighter. He releases my hand and goes to help my aunt, and I sit in the chair at the little square table and watch as they make spaghetti.

"So, Tristan, what do you think of my niece?" Aunt Rachel asks, playfully rubbing the top of my head as she passes me on her way to the pantry.

"She's the best friend I could ever ask for, Rachel," he says, smirking at me from behind the steam from the boiling pot. "Wish she was around a few years ago, but then that would be a different story, now wouldn't it?"

Aunt Rachel looks surprised, mouth slightly open and head cocked to the side. Her platinum blonde hair is stacked on top of her head, making her look like a tiny troll-doll with its outrageous style.

"I told her, Rachel. It's pretty hard to keep secrets from someone you're so much alike," he says, stirring the spaghetti. "Plus, it is better that she heard it from me, anyways.

"Well. I'm glad to see you two got so close so quickly," my aunt says as she's reaching into the cupboard to retrieve the plates. "Me, too," I chime in, smiling.

We sit at the table, and a feeling of ease washes over me. This is how it was supposed to be all along; this feeling of happiness should have been more present in my life.

"Oh, Katherine! I almost forgot, dear. You got a letter in the mail today from your mother. I suggest opening this one!" she says, trying to sound stern.

I fight the urge to roll my eyes. "Fine, I'll do it now so I don't forget. Be right back," I say as I stand and dramatically walk over to the counter, which is less than ten feet away. Aunt Rachel and Tristan laugh.

Tearing the letter open, my heart races. I don't know why, but it does.

■■■

Katherine,

You're lucky *I* opened the letter you sent your father. I burned it. Stop being foolish.

Mom.

My mouth drops open. I forgot all about the letter I sent! Anxiety rises up in me, my Punishment threatening to burst forth and set fire to my veins. I feel it, the buildup, but chase it away with deep breathing. A strong hand on the back of my neck relieves my anxiousness, and I look up to see a stunning set of blue eyes analyzing my every move.

"Everything alright, Katie?" he asks, humoring Rachel. He is good at masking his true feelings; his voice is so light, so innocent, that I raise my eyebrows in shock at his great lying skills.

"Uh, yeah! Yeah, it's all good," I say, playing along, not wanting to explain the letter in my hands.

"I should probably get home. It's weird, knowing we have school tomorrow. It feels like we were in a different world today," he says, so low my aunt can't hear.

"Yeah, I'll walk you out," I say, glancing at Aunt Rachel as I say so.

Tristan walks toward her before embracing her and whispering something. My aunt smiles and gives him a very maternal kiss on the cheek. As I said, she would be a fantastic mother if she would only settle down.

Walking Tristan to his car, I listen to the sounds of the nighttime, at peace despite knowing the information unearthed to me today.

He doesn't say anything, but takes my hands in his and pulls them up so they rest around his neck. *This is it. He's going to kiss me!* I think to myself.

But, he doesn't, and I'm feeling rejected and a little frustrated. He must feel this, because he chuckles and leans against his truck, pulling me against him. Our bodies are lined up from our shoulders to our feet, and I've never stood this close to a boy. Technically I have, but I feel like I've never been close to anyone before Tristan.

Wordlessly, he tilts my head up so that my eyes meet his, and he leans in. Keeps leaning… and tilts my head up more, so that I'm looking at the sky. I feel a light pressure on my neck just below my jaw, and my eyes flutter shut. A second later he stops, giving me a kiss on the forehead before gently moving me a few feet from his car. Dazed, I watch him get in, smile at me, and drive off. I just received the most passionate kiss I have ever received from a boy. And it wasn't even on my lips.

Later that night, as I lay into bed freshly showered with blow-dried hair, I look out my window. I think of David: what he's doing, where he is, what he's thinking… I know that he probably isn't the David I'm remembering, but a stranger. I conjure up a picture of him in my mind and think of a time where we sat under the stars on our roof and watched the fireworks on my birthday.

I'm not even sure if this memory is real, but it's bringing me comfort and, in some strange way, closure.

The stars glitter in the sky, twinkling like thousands of miniscule Christmas lights. The moon, bright and majestic, sits comfortably among the feathery clouds sitting stagnant in place. I pick the brightest star I can see, and do something usually reserved for children who see shooting stars; I make a wish. I wish for peace of mind, for happiness with Tristan, and for everything to fall into place. There are bigger problems in the world, but I risk sounding selfish if it means my wish comes true.

* * *

I'm dreaming again; my eyes must have closed but my brain is still whirring. I always seem to know when I'm dreaming, a gift David and I used to talk about frequently. This dream is the happiest I've had in a long time, filled with sunshine so real I can almost feel it warming my face. I'm wearing a floral dress that seems to glow in the brightness, and my hair is blowing in the light breeze, which smells like sea.

I'm in a park, barefoot, and the sun glints off a body of water, making me squint. I leisurely walk towards the rocks that line the shore; large, man-placed rocks to keep pedestrians from wandering into the surf. There is a bike path and dozens of picnic benches dotted around the large park, which stretches on and on parallel to the water.

I feel arms wrap around me, but I am not afraid; his presence is calming, and the lapping against the rocks makes for a picturesque moment. Turning, I find myself blinded by the beauty of Tristan's eyes, whose pupils are dilated in the bright light.

"Hey you," I say, which surprises me because I usually don't talk to people when I dream.

"Hey you," he says, smiling before tugging me towards the closest tree. "I have something to give you."

I smile, feeling free and happier than I ever remember being. Tristan reaches behind his neck, fingers moving gracefully as they unclasp a necklace I hadn't seen before. He removes it from its place, safely nestled under his shirt, and reaches for my hand. I lean against the tree as he braces his arms on either side of my head, against the rough bark. He takes my hand and his necklace dangles between our fingers, a silver cross hangs from the chain.

"I love you, Katie," he whispers, and then he leans in and kisses me.

Chapter 10

My alarm clock jolts me awake with its annoying buzzing, and I'm about to cry. The necklace, the water, the kiss... all a dream. I pound my fists into the bed, angry at the world for waking me up. I can tell it's going to be a bad day, but the sun already shining through my window begs to differ.

Putting on my school uniform, I hear my aunt bustling around the kitchen. I run a brush through my hair, put some mascara on and fix my skirt, which has a habit of riding up on my waist.

"Good morning, sweet pea! How'd you sleep?" Aunt Rachel says as she brushes flour off her face.

I giggle at the sight of the counter; covered in flour, it looks like a bomb hit.

"I slept great, Aunt Rachel," I say. My mood begins to lift as I watch my aunt smile at me in genuine happiness.

"Well that's great. You and I didn't get to talk very much after Trist left last night. Is there anything you wanna tell me?" she says, smirking in a knowing way only a woman can.

Hard as I try, I cannot stop the smile from spreading across my face. It starts off as a tiny, tight-lipped one, but grows into a full-on grin that Aunt Rachel has never seen me wear. Maybe she's some sort of magician, but Rachel seems to be the type of person that can coax a smile from anyone.

"He's a great young man," I say. Tristan can't be called a boy; the word is too immature to describe his character. "Guy" seems too unoriginal, but "young man" suits him so perfectly.

Aunt Rachel laughs, plopping a pancake onto my plate. "Nice to see you found a friend so soon. A week's time is all it took for you to get as close as you are? And, I'm not the snooping type, but I just so happened to see how close you got out by his truck," she winks.

I blush, which is ridiculous considering the fact that he didn't even kiss me on the lips. Although, a kiss on my neck is a lot more affectionate and it felt like the sky would open up and swallow us whole in a fiery inferno of passion. *Oh my gosh, I'm becoming such a teenager*, I think to myself with a giggle, which escapes my throat.

I look up to see my aunt smiling, struggling to contain laughter. "Well, I just want you two to be careful. A week might not seem that long to you, but moments of weakness can make anybody vulnerable," she says, but sees I'm confused and continues. "If you ever need, you know… protection? I keep some in the closet hallway. I'm not condoning that type of behavior, by any means, but better safe than sorry!"

My mouth pops open and I'm pretty sure my face was redder than the tomatoes growing in the garden out front. Tristan and I have known each other a week and she's already thinking…

"No, absolutely not, Aunt Rachel. Nope, nope, I'm good, thanks," I say, shoveling the last of my pancake into my mouth just as the doorbell dings.

"I'll get it, Katie. Go brush your teeth, you wouldn't want to keep the boyfriend waiting!" she calls loudly enough so that Tristan could probably hear her through the door.

She called him my boyfriend… is that what he is? We haven't really put a name to what we are, and I'm not sure there is one to describe us. He hasn't said we're officially a couple, but it's pretty much implied. Why would we see anybody else when we have each other right here?

"Have a good day, Katie!" Rachel calls to me from the kitchen as I make my way down the hallway. Tristan is sitting on the step, my backpack at his side. He looks especially nice today despite the sweater-vest that threatens to destroy his bad-boy image. Looking innocent and shy, he looks over his shoulder and stands when I close the door behind me.

"Hey you," he says, leaning over to kiss my cheek. I jump back, startled because this is what he said in my dream last night.

"Hey you," I say, smiling, hoping my dream will come true. Maybe the star heard my wish last night, and the dream is God's way of letting me know to expect good things. Or maybe I'm just reading too much into the entire thing; two words don't mean anything.

"Ready to get going?" he asks, tucking my hair behind my ear.

I smile wider, my mood completely improved. "Sure," I say as I bounce down the steps.

The ride to school is quiet, and the breeze blowing through the open truck windows feels nice on my face. Soft music is playing on the radio, so I reach over to turn it up and Lady Antebellum floats from the speakers. I hum along with the music, mouthing the words and tracing the scars on my wrists absentmindedly. I feel guilty, like I should be crying and depressed that David isn't who I thought he had become. But instead, I feel a peace and wholeness now that I know. Like maybe I can move on completely, free of the past and locked into the present.

"What are you thinking about?" I hear a velvet voice ask, breaking me from my thoughts.

I shake my head, not sure how to adequately put my feelings into words. "About how I think I should be depressed, about David, but how I'm feeling… normal," I say, voice breaking, contradicting my words.

Tristan cuts the engine in his usual parking space before reaching for my hand. "Let yourself feel whatever you feel. Don't second guess your emotions; they're there to show you how to continue. How to live. If they're telling you not to be upset, don't make yourself feel something else," he says, rubbing little circles on my hand with his thumb.

I smile and pull my hand away, climbing out of the car. The door bumps into something, and I instinctively pull it back, revealing a girl with short brown hair sprawled on the ground.

"Oh my gosh, I'm so sorry!" I say, shutting the door and nervously sticking my hands out to help her up. I watch her eyes shift from shocked to alarmed as she assesses my scarred wrists, and I pull my hands back, feeling guarded. "Are you okay?" I ask, wanting to avert her attention.

She nods, somewhat curtly, turns her head to pick up a book and stands. It is then I notice the bruising around her neck, which can't even be hidden by the white turtleneck under her uniform shirt. It's warm out today; she must be roasting in a long-sleeved shirt.

It hits me like a brick, the flashback. My father, standing over me as I cower, crying, on the floor of my closet. His hand snaps back, ready to strike my cheek, but he stopped, a heinous smile forming on his frightening face. I let out a sigh of relief, happy he was appeased with merely frightening me at the time.

But I should have known better. Both of his meaty hands shot forward, one tilting my head back so that I was staring at the ceiling and one wrapped around my neck. Squeezing, squeezing, until I saw stars and my world faded to black.

I must have been staring at the girl too long, because she squirms and walks around me, feet shuffling on the asphalt. I hear horns honking and kids shouting and these sounds snap me back to reality. My cheeks burn and I feel like his hands are still on my throat. I turn my head to find Tristan watching the brown haired girl retreat across the parking lot, and my eyes catch something shimmering in the sunlight. A bracelet. I bend down and pick it up, observing the charms with curiosity. A pair of angel wings graces the intricate silver chain, along with a set of ballet shoes, and a butterfly.

Carefully, I put the bracelet in the pocket of my skirt, knowing I'll track down the brown haired girl later to see if it belongs to her.

"That's Sorena Murray. She and I used to be really good friends, but then I…" Tristan trails off, letting his words float into the air.

"Sorena. I like that name," I say, biting my lip.

"I used to call her Sorren, but she complained that it was too masculine," he chuckles, eyes distant.

"Why haven't I seen her before? I have a hard time believing she would've gone on the Greece trip," I say as we start walking through the parking lot, swerving through the spaces of parked cars.

Tristan shrugs, letting his hand find mine. "I don't know, she seems like a totally different person than who I knew. What did you pick up?"

I release his hand, watching his face fall ever so slightly, and fish into my pocket for the bracelet. "This was on the ground. It's probably Sorren's, but I'm not positive," I say, handing it to him.

He smiles, nodding. "It's hers. She used to wear this all the time. I bought her the star charm for her fourteenth birthday. She had a freaky obsession with fate and Greek gods."

For a moment, jealousy races through me at the thought of Tristan having a girlfriend. Malaya had said he was popular among the girls in school, but I hadn't even given it a second thought. He's a different person now, but I'll ask him about it later out of simple curiosity.

"Did you date her?" I ask, some of the jealousy seeping into my words, which makes me feel horrible. The poor girl looked like a scared little doe, and I had the nerve to feel aggravation towards her?

He laughs slightly, putting the bracelet back into my pocket before grasping my hand again. Little tings of electricity shoot through my skin, and I feel definite smugness that I'm holding his hand. If the people in this school can't see what kind of person Tristan really is, they don't deserve our attention.

"No, Katie. Sorren and I never dated. She's, well… she's been my friend since we were toddlers. I've only ever seen her as my childhood friend. That's why I'm so shocked she never tried to contact me," he says, sadness weighing his words down.

I give him a sad little smile and squeeze his hand before tugging him towards our first period class. About fifteen minutes into the class, I raise my hand, asking to use the bathroom. The hallways are painted a dull yellow, which doesn't cease to remind me of the smoke-stained walls of my father's study back in Chicago. My tiny black high-heeled shoes thwack against the gray tile as I make my way to the girls bathroom at the end of the hall.

As I open the door, I'm greeted by a familiar face. Malaya stands before me, big lips freshly coated with pink gloss.

"Hi, Katherine," she says, voice brimming with false niceness.

"Malaya," I say, voice matching her fake tone.

"I think we started off on the wrong foot… why don't we just forget all words exchanged between us and start fresh," she continues, smiling like a Girl Scout trying to convince you to buy twenty boxes of cookies.

I wish the world worked that way. Being able to start anew with no biases, hostility, or leeriness would probably bring about world peace. If Malaya thinks I'm going to disregard her nasty demeanor and hurtful words, she's out of her mind. But I can at least try to be a friendly acquaintance, because enemies are really the last things I need at the moment. Yes, acquaintanceship is okay, but I'll tread lightly.

"Of course. I really don't want to miss Gov, so would you excuse me?" I say, inching past her.

She smiles, white teeth contrasting against her dark skin. "Sure. I'll see you around!"

I hear muffled sniffling noises echoing in the tiny bathroom so I crouch to see what stall the crying girl is hiding in. The room is silent, empty of occupants except for me and the crier.

"Hello?" I say in a cooing voice usually reserved for the horses when I'm trying not to spook them.

The crying stops and I realize she must not have heard me enter the bathroom. Scenes of "Moaning Myrtle" from Harry Potter flash through my mind, and I suppress an extremely inappropriate laugh.

"Hey, what's wrong?" I ask, standing in front of the stall. Unexpectedly, the door flies open, smacking me in the shoulder before slamming against the wall.

My eyes meet Sorren's, which are a peculiar shade of blue, and I gasp when I see the anger on her face. Her eyes are makeup free, but framed with thick, dark lashes that any Covergirl would die for. My mouth hangs open slightly, showing my shock, and I snap it closed, immediately on the defensive. Her posture is different than it was in the parking lot, emanating strength and hardness.

"Just *leave me alone*," she enunciates the last three words, sounding desperate.

"I just want to see if you're alright," I say, becoming angered at her change in character. Maybe she has an alter ego...

She tries to push past me, but my hand shoots out to grasp her arm, instinctively trying to offer her some form of comfort. A suction-like feeling spreads through my arm, gluing my hand to her in an unnatural way. I feel a soft nudge in my mind, telling me to relax, and my eyes shut.

* * *

I'm standing in a darkened hall, pressed against cool bricks. A girl races past me, wearing old-fashioned clothing: a light blue dress, short white gloves, and a hat that tipped to one side. I feel trapped, like my mind is detached from the body it's in. I hear thoughts overlapping my own. Attempting to calm down and listen to what the voice is saying, I say a quick prayer and take a deep breath.

I start walking down the hallway and the thoughts get louder as I concentrate on them. *"Where are you? Please tell me you're alright. Dear God, let him be alright."* I hear in my head, and the voice sounds like my own, if not for the southern twang.

I open the door, and the smells of cigars and whiskey hit my nose. Music is playing, but not from a stereo. A band is playing in the corner of what looks like a bar in someone's basement. The men around me have blurred faces, but their clothing is from the roaring twenties era. Men play cards on the floor, wagering cigarettes and chewing tobacco.

"Katherine!" I hear a voice call, and I turn my head, relief spreading through the body at the sight of… Sorren?

"Cassandra! Where's Tristan? Is he alright?" the girl asks in succession, my voice sounding foreign thanks to the thick accent. The thoughts swirling through my head were jumbling together, making my brain actually hurt.

The rushing girl is me. She looks like me, straight down to the slightly crooked bottom teeth. The girl looks like she's from a different time, just like everyone else in the room. She exudes strength and sassiness and sports a southern accent, but she is me. Her eyes graze past my own and it is in that moment that I know I was once the girl standing before me.

"He's outside with your brother. We're tryin' to find a way to git 'im and you up North, in case this don't blow over," Sorren says, voice shaking.

"What was he thinkin' comin' to a place like this right now?!" she exclaimed, drawing attention to her and Sorren.

"Adrian said to meet 'im here outside. What in the Lord's name are you doin' here? It's dangerous for you, too!"

Katherine's eyes roll, which makes me smile knowing this is exactly the reaction I would have if someone had asked me that question today.

"Who cares what I'm doin' here! Let's git outside and drag that boy home," Katherine said, grabbing her friends forearm. As soon as the body's hand touched Sorren's skin, I was jolted back into the present.

* * *

My mind felt like it was being sucked through a vacuum, the sensation unpleasant. I open my eyes and find myself sitting on the bathroom floor with my head against the wall under the sink. Sorren is a few feet away, staring at me with an expression no less than terrified. She saw it too, then? The vision? What was it, exactly? I feel a ting of frustration for having this extra burden tossed onto my shoulders right now.

"What the hell *are* you, some kind of freak?!" she asks with contempt I'm not accustomed to being the subject of.

"I should ask you the same question!" I reply because I'm not exactly sure how to respond.

"You did see that, didn't you?"

"No, I'm sitting over here 'cause the view's *great,*" I say, gesturing to the graffiti filled door a few feet in front of me.

"Shut up Katherine! Tell me what you saw!" Sorren yells, and I shush her before a teacher catches wind of our conversation and steps in.

"It looked like a… speakeasy. You know, those illegal bars in the twenties?" She nods, looking more frightened with my every word. "It was you and me talking about-"

"Tristan and someone named Adrian. Yup, got that. Seriously, what are you? Some kind of psychic? I had a dream just like this. Last night, I dreamt that you and Tristan were sitting at an old kitchen table- with me- eating corn. What the hell?! That is *not* a coincidence!" she cries, tears forming in her eyes.

I climb to my feet, carefully avoiding smacking my head on the sink. "Sorren, don't. We're obviously supposed to work it out together-"

"How do you know? If you're supposedly just as confused as I am, how do you know this isn't some sort of freaky ghost telepathic thing…" she cuts herself off, looking aggravated.

Just then, a girl walks into the bathroom. I catch her eye and she smiles, mouth full of red rubber bands. It's the smiling girl from my English class, from the back row. I smile back, but it's contrived and she knows it. A look of confusion passes over her face as she looks at Sorren's crying form and my shaking hands. Without a word, she walks back into the hallway, sending me a silent *"hope everything's okay"* look with her eyes.

"Look, this obviously isn't the place to chat about this. Why don't we get together after school and talk then?"

She scoffs. "You're seriously going to walk through the halls and act like none of that even happened? Do you not feel *anything?* I'm legit about to piss myself right now!"

That caught me off guard. I've never thought of myself as unfeeling. It's sort of ironic, actually.

"Do you want me to take you to the nurse? Maybe she'll send you home?" I ask, attempting to act like I wasn't seriously shocked by her accusation.

"Hell no, I'm not going anywhere without you. Right now, I know you're as crazy as me. So either you ditch with me willingly or I will rip this mirror off the wall, smash it and we'll both get in school suspension. Either way, you're explaining this. Now," she says, trying to look rough and tough but the tears flowing from her eyes admit how afraid she still is.

"Okay. We just walk out?" I ask, unsure of how to proceed. I don't want to make a bad impression with my semi-new teachers, and ditching barely a month into their classes is a horrible idea. But I want to know what's going on as much, if not more so, than Sorren does.

"If you want, call your parents and have them give their permission to let you leave. The principal will let you do that, if you say you're not feeling well. And that wouldn't be a hard lie to pull off, 'cause you're kind of green, Kath," she says.

The nickname surprises me, and apparently her, too. But I take her advice and call Rachel, telling her I don't really feel well and that I'm coming home after fourth period. I feel bad about lying to her, because I'm really leaving right now, barely second period, but there's more important matters on my hands.

We get in Sorren's car and I send a quick message to Tristan, my fingers fumbling with the keys. I hate text messaging.

Skipping rest of day. I'm fine. Call me when you're out of your last class.

I figure he'll check his phone during the class change, so I plop it back in my pocket, not wanting to be tempted to ask him to skip with us. School is important to him and skipping would dig at his conscience. At least, that's what I'm telling myself. Part of me knows this vision ends badly, although I don't know how. And I want Sorren and me to figure it out before we involve Tristan.

"Okay, so what do you know that you're not telling me?" Sorren asks after she orders two coffees from the Starbucks drive-through window. I had asked her why bother stopping for coffee, and she said she needs some extra energy.

I debate telling her about my encounter with God, but honestly, feel very protective of it. I don't even know this girl, but my heart is telling me I can trust her. However, my stomach is churning.

"I'm going to keep this brief, because it isn't something I share with strangers, okay? I need you to believe me when I tell you that I'm not lying. This won't make any sense to you if you don't trust me," I say, voice taking on a serious tone.

"I'm pretty sure I'll believe anything at this point, Kath," she says, laughing once.

So I tell her the very basics of my story, hoping it will be enough to calm her a bit.

"Let me make sure I got everything: you died, you somehow came back to life. But what does Tristan have to do with that?" she asks the one question I don't want to answer.

"Tristan and I... have a history together," which isn't all together untrue. It's very vague, yes, but not untrue.

She scoffs. "I've known that boy since we were in diapers and he's never said a word about you before. I've been in New York for the past two weeks, I come home and here you are, staple gunned to his side and he's nothing like he was before he left. I don't know exactly what there is between you two, but I think you need to tell me."

I feel a surge of defiance and the words are out of my mouth before I can stop them. "Look, I don't need to tell you anything I don't want to tell you. You think I have your answers but I don't have them all, and some you have no right knowing!"

Sorren looks somewhat impressed. "I took you as the pushover type, Kath. Looks like nothing is impossible," she laughs to herself.

"So you think God had something to do with what we saw today?" Sorren continues, sounding skeptical.

"Well... yeah. He has something to do with everything, but what we saw gave me the same feeling that I had when I"- I was going to say "when I saw Tristan in my vision," but I caught myself.

"When you what?"

"When I came back to life," I fill in, absentmindedly touching my wrists. Remembering.

"I'll be honest here, sweetheart, I'm not feelin' it," she says, sipping her iced coffee.

"You don't believe me? Or you don't believe in God?" I ask, feeling uncomfortable.

"I don't know what I believe in anymore. But I can't deny that our little vision thing freaked me *the hell out.*"

"Do you think it was real? Like Him showing us something that happened to us in the past? Maybe they were our relatives or something," I say, my inquisitive side becoming frustrated and even more curious.

"Now I'm second guessing if you saw what I did. If you think for a second that it wasn't us in that vision, you're insane. They'd have to be our twins," she says, pulling onto the somewhat busy street.

"I'm just taking a shot in the dark here, Sorren! What do you think it was?" I exclaim, exasperated.

"How the hell should I know? You're the friggin' prodigy over there!"

I roll my eyes, but strangely feel the urge to laugh. *Really* laugh. I feel calm about the entire situation, which leads me to believe that God is telling me not to fret over it. But why would he show us that if we weren't meant to figure it out? Maybe the answer is right in front of us, and we just don't see it. Maybe we're too blind to know what and who we truly are, which is a major fault of humanity. Divine intervention opened my eyes, but we should all be able to see our true potential on our own.

"Hello? You awake over there?" a sarcastic voice asks, shocked to see that we were parked in front of Rachel's house.

"How did you know where I live?" I ask, shocked.

She winks. "I have my ways. But gossip gets around and believe me when I say the rumor mill spun when it heard that Miss. Rachel was gettin' a kid."

I felt the sudden temptation to ask her to come in, to hang out like any normal teenagers skipping school would. Sure, Rachel might be pissed if she found out, but then again she may be happy to see me "adjusting."

"Do you want to come inside?" I ask, my voice hitching at the end, embarrassingly enough.

"It depends if you have a bathroom, because I really need to use one," she laughs.

I roll my eyes jokingly. "No, Sorren. We pee in the woods."

She laughs, snorting as she does so. "I think you and I are gonna be great friends," she says, slamming the car door behind her.

Chapter 11

Sorren and I spent the rest of the day chatting in the living room about seemingly insignificant things. However, our conversation was anything but. It was like I could feel my wounds being sewed together again; the veins that were ripped apart by betrayal and abuse had already been patched up thanks to Tristan and Aunt Rachel, in an astounding amount of time. But with Sorren, I had the one thing I've always dreamed of but never been good enough to have. A friend.

Sure, lots of therapists and doctors have used the word to cajole me into a happier state of mind, but I've never known the meaning of the word until today. It's as if our souls are connected, helping us bond and forget about everything but petty teenage drama. I never in a million years thought that my scars and wounds could be healed so quickly, but it goes to show you that anything is possible when you're surrounded by people who so obviously care about you.

When my phone chimes at twelve o'clock, just after the fourth period bell would have rang, I would have ignored it if not for the contact name on the little glowing screen.

"Hi," I say, wiping the tears from underneath my eyes. We had been laughing at a story Sorren told, but my tears are filled with many different emotions, all of which are just as they should be.

"Katie, where are you? Are you alright?" Tristan asked, sounding disturbed.

I frown, the bubble of ignorance that had surrounded me popping. It was nice to ignore my problems for one afternoon, but a mystery still remains and it's as haunting as ever.

"Tristan, I'm fine. Sorren and I are at my house, just talking. I think that, maybe, you should come over instead of me having to explain this over the phone," I say, headache ensuing.

"Your house with *Sorren?*" He says, sounding baffled.

I smile, but when I remember that he can't see me, I stop, feeling stupid. "Yeah, she's right next to me."

He took that as a cue to not say anything deprecating, and instead of asking further questions like I predicted he would, he informs me that he'll be over in ten minutes.

~ 173 ~

"You ever heard of the word 'codependent?'" Sorren asks, dead serious.

"Yeah, and it doesn't apply to Tristan and I so don't even say so," I refute.

"You two are the talk of the school right now. How you never go anywhere without the other, how you spend every second of every day together, yadda yadda yadda," she makes hand gestures as she speaks, trying to prove her point.

"First of all, basically the entire student body has been overseas for the entire time I've known Tristan. How would they know how we act outside of school? Which, by the way, we aren't with each other 'every second of every day,'" I say, which is true. Minus the past few days, we've only ever seen one another in school.

"Okay. I believe you over those gossiping lemmings I've had to tolerate for almost my entire life. I have a question, though. How did you meet him?"

That's an easy one. "The first day of school. I didn't see you that day."

She nods, seemingly thinking about something. "You met the first day of school and you're already this serious about him?" she asks, raising one pierced eyebrow. "Do you even know about his life? What he's been through?"

This makes my temper flare, which is ridiculous because there's no way she could possibly understand our situation. "Our relationship isn't serious. I don't even know what to call it; we haven't put a name to what we are. And yes, I do know about his life, actually. Where have you been for the past two years?" I ask the last question carefully, with just enough venom to let her know I want a serious, legit answer.

"Yeah, Sorren. Where have you been for the past two years?" asks a beautiful voice from behind me.

The atmosphere seems to buzz with electricity, but not the awkward kind. Not the normal kind you'd feel in a situation like this. It's a whirring that you can almost physically see rippling across the stale air of the air conditioned house, and it feels almost supernatural.

Sorren's eyes widen before she regains her composure. "Where should I have been, Trist? You weren't you anymore," she says, voice devoid of any hostility or anger. In fact, she sounds desperate.

"If you had answered my letters you'd have known that I *was* myself again!" he exclaims, and it's the first time I've ever heard him raise his voice.

I sit on the couch, sinking into the cushions as they stare at one another, each one refusing to break the heavy silence. I'm about to draw attention to the buzzing atmosphere when suddenly, Sorren stands up and runs across the tiny room to Tristan, hugging him the way a little girl would hug her father after a bad day at school.

Tristan looks directly into my eyes before returning the hug. I look at my hands, playing with my fingers in my lap, tracing the ugly scars on my wrists that seem to fade a little more each day. I'd be lying if I didn't say I feel a twinge of jealousy and subtle defensiveness towards Sorren for so blatantly embracing Tristan, but I shake off the ridiculous feeling.

"I'm sorry. I'm so, so sorry I wasn't there for you. You were just so... mean," Sorren says, and I realize she's crying. She's a thick-skinned person, not the crying type; for her to break down twice in one day must be a record.

"I'm sorry. I told you that in every letter I sent you, but I just stopped writing after a while. I feel like everything I did, everything I said, never happened," he says in a quiet voice.

"Well it did. And you were a dick for a long time," Sorren says, pulling away. "But I miss you. *You*, not that other guy who wigged out before disappearing for two years."

"Why didn't you open my letters? You were that angry with me?" he asks.

Sorren wipes her nose, and I stand before walking down the hallway into the bathroom. I feel like I was seriously encroaching on a heart-to-heart conversation between two long lost friends, and I used any excuse I could to leave the room. Dampening a cloth with cool water, I take it and a handful of tissues to Sorren, handing them to her before going into the kitchen. Everything seems to be moving in slow motion.

Tristan grabs my hand as I pass, preventing me from leaving. He must see something in my expression, because his face turns shocked.

"Katherine? Katherine?" he says, shaking my shoulders gently but firmly.

My head starts swaying, and the buzzing in the atmosphere becomes annoyingly loud. My vision blurs and I can tell I'm about to lose consciousness. Tristan scoops me up with ease and carries me over to the couch, laying my head in his lap, pushing my hair back and pressing the damp cloth I had gotten for

Sorren to my forehead. She stands over me with a frightened expression.

"Shit, is she gonna pass out?" Sorren asks, her voice echoing in my head like she yelled her words into the Grand Canyon.

"She better not. Can you grab her some water?" the words reverberate, crashing against my skull in a painful cadence.

"Sweetheart, look at me. Do you want me to take you to the hospital?" Tristan asks, dabbing cool water on my face with his hands.

My eyes flutter and I think I hear a voice and see faces but I'm not sure because everything is swaying and all I can think is "I'm scared." Tristan presses his lips to my forehead and the pain and fear and dizzying blurriness halts immediately.

"Woah, that was beyond strange," I say, blinking repeatedly as Tristan leans back, giving me space to breathe. I go to sit up, but he pushes me down.

"Katie, I think you should lie down. I don't mind being your pillow," he smiles sweetly, but I can see the worry in his blue eyes.

"I think she's had her full of craziness today, Tristan. Why don't we let her stay here and you and I can go outside. I'll explain everything to him, Kath," Sorren says, patting my knee.

"You really think leaving her alone right now is a good idea?" Tristan asks rhetorically.

"No, I feel fine now. Honestly, Tristan. I wouldn't lie to you," I say, sitting up. Instead of lingering pain or fatigue, I'm refreshed and more awake than I was before this dramatic little episode. "Can you explain everything, Sorren? I'm going to go… wash my face." My excuse is silly, but I know that with Tristan here I won't be able to hold in my speculations about the vision with Sorren.

"Do you need help walking there? I can stay with you," Tristan offers, helping me up by taking both of my hands in a steady grip.

"No, I'm alright. Really, Tristan, don't worry about me," I smile, squeezing his hands.

"I'll always worry about you," he says, and I get locked in his gaze like some cliché heroin in a romance novel.

Sorren clears her throat theatrically loud and I pull my hands away from Tristan's, heading to the bathroom. I hear them walk out the front door and I splash my face with cool water and stare at my reflection.

Two months ago, I'd have cringed. I would've stared at the blonde-haired green-eyed girl in the mirror and thought, *"Who are you?"* I would've despised my few freckles dotting my nose, which my old boyfriend made fun of so often. My eyes would've welled up with tears thinking of the taunts from the girls at school about my slightly crooked bottom teeth and tiny spots of acne.

A lot can happen in two months. As I look in the mirror, I still think *"Who are you?"* but I think it with curiosity. Inquisitiveness as to who I will become, and what I am capable of. Bouts of insecurity and fear and loneliness and regret still harbor places in my mending heart, but today, my green eyes brighten with the knowledge that I'm not alone anymore.

A figure moves behind me in the mirror, and I see the heavenly blue eyes I was blessed to have sent to me. His arms wrap around my waist and his chin rests on my shoulder, cheek touching mine. The stance and embrace is intimate, but instead of being seductive, it's comforting and innocent.

"Have I ever told you that you're beautiful?" he says, his breath tickling my cheek.

I watch my reflection smile as I gently move my arms around his neck, returning the embrace. "You might've mentioned it before. I can't remember," I say.

"I don't ever want you to forget it. You're beautiful."

The warmth in his tone sends peaceful shivers down my body, and I want nothing more than to freeze time in this moment; to avoid discussing the unknown or the past or the future. But that is a dreamers reality, and mine is much different.

"Sorren told you, right?" I say, breaking the spell.

Tristan sighs and stands to his full height, breaking our encirclement. "Yes, but I want to know what you really think. She didn't mention anything about us... *looking* for one another. I didn't tell her, but I was wondering why you didn't. It's not important right now, but I'm curious because you told her everything else."

I look away from our reflections and turn to face the real thing, and I realize that the last time I saw him in a bathroom, he killed himself. The thought turns my blood to ice and I swallow, hard, to keep the bile from rising. Thinking of *that* literally makes my stomach churn.

"Can we go in my room?" I ask, wanting to leave the bathroom as soon as possible.

"Absolutely," he says, leading me to the room that was once his.

I move past him to sit on the bed, my back against the headboard. Tristan looks conflicted; like he isn't sure I was okay with him sitting.

"You can sit down, ya know. We're home alone, and even if we weren't, we're just talking," I say, giggling.

He immediately complies, sitting at me knees, facing me.

My giggling turns into a huff of irritation. How I long to be able to sit on my bed with Tristan without all this heavy talk weighing us down.

"I didn't tell Sorren about how I was looking for you because I feel… weirdly protective of that information; like I'm not supposed to share it with anyone. Do you feel that way?" I ask, sounding like a therapist asking *"And how do you feel about that?"*

He nods, eyes brightening. "I feel that way, too. I felt this weird tugging in my head, when I was about to tell her; like I'm not supposed to let her know. Tell me what you think of that vision, of you and Sorren."

My eyebrows knit together, unsure of how to put my feelings into words. "I felt really connected to the body I was in, Tristan; like I was remembering things I've forgotten. Almost as if... it was a dream that I could never quite remember. But I couldn't control the body's actions. I was myself, though. I saw my reflection in the dirty mirror on the wall. And I called Sorren Cassandra. Your name was mentioned, and some guy named Adrian," I stop talking when Tristan's face pales a shade. "What?"

"Katie, I've been having dreams, every night, about a man named Adrian. I always wake up frightened, but nothing ever happens in the dreams. I just know he's looking for me," he says, looking genuinely freaked out. I don't know what to say, and Tristan must know this because he urges me to continue.

"I was really afraid. Not *me* me, but the body I was in. Which was mine... it's hard to explain, but my feelings and thoughts were overlapping with those of the 'twenties me.' Do you understand? Am I making sense?" I say, getting frustrated with my lack of couth in my explanation.

"Yes, it makes sense. But what were *you* feeling when this was happening?"

I open my mouth, but then shut it again, because I'm not sure how to answer. I had wanted to be afraid, but I wasn't. "I thought the only rational reaction was to be afraid. But I wasn't, I just knew I should've been, so I convinced myself that I was scared. I was… relieved; like a burden was lifted off my shoulders upon seeing what I saw."

"What did you feel like twenty minutes ago? When you were about to pass out?"

"I was scared. My vision blurred and my head hurt like hell, but when you kissed my forehead, it all stopped as if a switch was turned off."

Tristan takes on his *"I'm deep in thought"* look, but I don't think either of us has a perfect explanation for what happened today.

"Should we just stop trying to figure it out and let it explain itself? Stop speculating and wait until God wants us to know more?" I suggest.

He nods, eyes meeting mine. "There's not much more we *can* do, is there?"

We sit in unsatisfied silence, the unknown looming over our heads like a dark cloud.

"Let's pray over it, tonight. Before we each go to bed, mention it. Not now; let's just let it rest for now," he says, moving his hands as he speaks.

I nod, pulling my knees up to my chest, feeling the soft material of the gray sweatpants I changed into when I arrived home. I don't like the feeling of mystery on my shoulders, and I'm sure my face is compressed into a frown.

I move, getting under the covers and laying down as if I were going to sleep.

"Come on," I motion for Tristan to join me, so he does. He climbs under the covers, careful not to jostle me, and we lay there, facing one another, eye to eye.

"What's your favorite band?" I ask, continuing our game of "truth" from two weeks ago. He chuckles, remembering how we never did get to finish.

"Band or solo singer?" he asks, smirking.

"Both."

He thinks for a moment before saying, "My favorite band is Young the Giant. My favorite solo artist is Keith Urban. I'm a country fan, you know that, but I listen to practically anything. What's your worst fear?"

"Mmm... are we being heavy or light?" I say, referring to the weight of our conversation.

"Light," he says immediately.

"Okay. I'm terrified of heights. Even walking up a staircase makes my heart pound and hands shake." I'm happy we're playing the light version, because my worst fear would definitely put another damper on the day.

What I'm truly afraid of, what I had to write my English essay on, is that I would've died the day I tried to kill myself. It's in the past, but I dread ever feeling that way again. So worthless, so full of self-hatred and guilt over driving my brother away and disappointing my parents and forcing them to lash out at me. That's what my parents made me feel; guilty. They pinned all their problems on me, and I was so brainwashed by self-loathing that I grew to agree with them. Ultimately, I went to kill myself because I truly believed I was worthless. Irrational, misplaced guilt motivated me, and it clung to me like suction cups.

"Baby?" I hear a warm voice say, bringing me out of my own thoughts. I blink repeatedly, casting away the memories.

"Sorry," I say, and I'm surprised to feel warm tears running down my face.

Tristan wipes the tears away, giving me the comfort and reassurance I've never felt before. His touch is so tender, so light yet so compassionate and kind, I feel the desperate urge to kiss him.

So I do. I kiss his palm, turning my head to do so. My lips barely touch his skin when I see a figure standing in the doorway. With eyebrows raised, hands on hips, lips curved into an amused smirk, my aunt watches us.

I screech, a knee-jerk reaction to seeing a looming figure in a place you didn't expect to see one. Tristan jolts like he'd been stabbed, head banging against the headboard in the process.

"Aunt Rachel! What are you doing home?" I sputter so fast it's a miracle she understood me.

"You told me that you'd be home after fourth period. It's almost one-thirty, so I came home early to make sure you're alright," she says, sounding stern, which is frightening.

"I'm feeling fine now! It's been a rough day and Tristan is done with his classes by noon. Did you know he's so ahead in his school work that he only goes for a half day? Isn't that inspiring? He's such a good influence," I blabber, which would have made Tristan laugh if he didn't look so afraid.

"I'm not your mother, Katherine. I trust you. If you wanna lay in bed talkin' with your boyfriend, you go right ahead. Just keep it to talkin' and I won't bother you about it. Nice to see your face today, Trist. I'm so happy you kids are together; it's like fate made it so," she says, leaning against the doorframe.

The entire situation is kind of funny: I'm in my bed, under the covers with a boy, and my aunt is telling us how happy she is about it. Unexpectedly, I start laughing. *Really* laughing, which causes my stomach to hurt because it's sore from all the hysterical heaving I experienced when talking with Sorren in the living room. It isn't until I start snorting, albeit a dainty, tiny snort, that Tristan starts laughing with me. I throw my head back, hitting the headboard as I do so, which makes me laugh even more.

Aunt Rachel just stares at us with a peaceful expression and I think I see tears fill her eyes, but I can't be sure because I'm laughing so hard. Tristan's laugh is graceful, even for a boy, and it sends a sense of tranquility through my veins. Somehow, we end up under the covers again, his arm under my head, the other slung across my side, keeping me tight against him. And it's in this moment that I know. This moment, following an absurd laughing fit and an insanely crazy day, means more to me than anything ever has.

With his breathing in sync with mine, I trace little circles on his soft uniform polo shirt. His eyes are closed, but I know he's still awake because he's tracing circles on my back. It's been barely a month and I trust Tristan more than I've ever trusted anyone before. We're connected like no one else, through our essence and our minds. It is in this moment that I realize what my soul seems to have known since the beginning; I love him.

I felt like I knew him the moment we met, and like I knew him even more so when he told me his story. But now, here, I feel like I know Tristan for who he is; not an angel the Lord sent to ease my pain, or a boy I saw in a vision... No, right now Tristan is a boy who is my best friend: kind and loyal and respectful and funny. Tristan is a boy who just so happens to be my Divine match, but I don't have these feelings because I *should* or am *obliged* too.

I have these feelings because I *want* to. I don't love him because God told me to. I love him for who he is. And it is in this moment that another piece of my mending heart heals itself.

■ ■

That night, as I lie in bed, my thoughts threaten to overtake the calm surrounding me. As Tristan and I agreed, I pick up my phone and call him to let him know I'm turning in for the night. It rings a few times, then a musical voice answers.

"Hey. You turning in?"

"Yup. Why'd you want me to call you?" I ask. He made me promise to call him before I went to bed, but never said why.

"I… just wanted your voice to be the last I hear before I go to bed. Maybe I'll have more pleasant dreams," he says meekly, and I can picture him blushing as he catches the double meaning behind his words.

I laugh, forcing myself to keep it quiet. "Well goodnight, then. I'll see you tomorrow, Tristan. Sweet dreams."

"Goodnight, Katie."

And we hang up, a smile still on my face. I can definitely see how others who are unaware of our situation would accuse me and Tristan of being a codependent couple, but with all the facts, you'd see that we're just happy to be with one another.

My eyes grow heavy, but a buzzing sensation starts pulsing in the back of my head. At first I think it's just a headache, but it intensifies. I slowly get out of bed with the intention of getting a Tylenol from the bathroom cupboard. My feet drag, and my head spins, but now I'm standing in the hallway. It was stupid to get up, but I don't think I would've been able to call to Rachel if I hadn't of.

"Katherine, honey? Do you need something?" I hear my aunt ask, but the buzzing overtakes my ears just like it did this afternoon. "Katherine!" she exclaims.

And then I fall to the floor, eyes rolling to the back of my head. But this time, I am not afraid.

I hear the voices before I'm aware of anything else. It's like my senses are slowly being brought into focus one at a time. I can feel a cool floor below me, and realize I'm lying on my stomach. My eyes pop open and I find myself in the same speakeasy that I found myself in earlier. Thankfully, I'm not trapped in the body again.

I stand, taking in my surroundings. I see myself come around a corner of the basement bar, and Sorren strolls out from behind a table, looking perturbed. They exchange words, the conversation I've already over heard, before making their way up a small staircase and opening a door. I jog after them, refusing to be left behind. It's nighttime, but the moon is so full that it illuminates the surrounding area. I can see every line and crevice that sits on the land, and about thirty feet from where I'm standing, "me," "Sorren/Cassandra," and Tristan stand, accompanied by... my brother.

I stop in my tracks, breath hitching and pulse thundering. David looks so... different. His hand reaches out to

Sorren/Cassandra and she takes it. Their mouths are moving, so I waste no more time and rush over to where they stand. Tristan, though older looking in this vision, is just as striking as he is today, but instead of blueness in his eyes, they look gray, bleached by the moonlight.

"We can't stand around here, out in the open. Not at a place like this. Why in God's name did you come here, Tristan?" "I" asked, tears flowing from my eyes.

He walked over to "me," taking me in his arms as I gripped him fiercely. "I'm innocent, my love. Innocent until proven otherwise. Adrian had to stop by to speak to a colleague, so I tagged along. The better question is what on Earth were you thinkin' followin' me to a place like this?" he asks, his southern accent not as pronounced as mine was.

"If you thought I was jus' gonna sit by while you went and got yourself killed, you've lost your mind," my doppelganger replied vehemently. "I know you didn't kill that man, but someone went through an awful lot of trouble blamin' it on you. This is the mob we're dealing with, Tristan! Use your head!"

Tristan sighed before kissing "me" and placing a hand on my stomach. "You know you shouldn't act so foolish, love. You're carryin' precious cargo, angel."

I just stand here during this entire exchange, watching the expressions on everyone's faces. Sorren/Cassandra looks pained, but smiles at the mention of a baby. My brother stood there with an indifferent look on his face, but alternated between staring at the ground and at Sorren.

"Let's get home, Tristan. Please," I had said to him, touching his cheek with my left hand. A ring glinted off my ring finger and off Tristan's as well.

"Adrian, take us home will you? Do your business another night, friend. My wife is frightened," Tristan said, not taking his eyes off me.

Sorren/Cassandra entered the very early looking car first, and Adrian motioned for "me" to enter as well. Just as I was climbing into the car, his arm shot out, hand wrapping around my neck. Present-day "me" gasped, and I walked even closer to the group, heart pounding but still feeling unafraid.

"Adrian! What are you doing?" Tristan yelled, moving to grab me, but Adrian had pressed a knife to my throat, stopping Tristan in his tracks. "You dirty traitor. It's been you all along, hasn't it! You framed me for Callie's murder!"

My brother/Adrian just laughed a brutal, unfeeling cackle that transformed his face into that of a madman. It was an expression I had only seen once on his face: when I witnessed one of his lapses in reality, before he was sent away.

"You gave me no choice, Tristan! You think I don't know what you say about me? The whole county thinks I'm crazy! You've always had it all, been so sure of yourself all the time, well who's in control now?!" the madman screams, lacking the southern accent the other three possessed, pressing the knife further into the throat of the mom-to-be.

Sorren started crying from inside the car, curling into a ball. I see bruises on her legs as the skirt of her dress rides up, and I'm at a loss of words. Something clicks in my head, divine intervention probably, and I know that this Adrian, this madman who I know is my present-day brother, beats Cassandra, his wife, to a pulp weekly. Watching this unfold, detached from my emotions so I can comprehend everything, I feel like I'm resurfacing from a dream. But the scene stays put, and I continue to watch.

"Adrian, Katherine doesn't deserve your rage. I understand that I do, but you don't need to punish her, to punish our child, for my mistakes," Tristan said firmly.

"I loved her! You took her from me, like you took everything else! It would hurt you more if I killed her and left you a cripple," Adrian growled.

~ 194 ~

By then, the struggling Katherine in Adrian's arms had started sobbing, growing limp and screaming when he pressed the knife in further, drawing blood. Tristan looked conflicted, debating whether or not to tackle Adrian to the ground and risk his wife getting injured, or to keep trying to talk some sense into him. One look in his friends' eyes told him that he was beyond saving, so Tristan lunged.

A strangled sob came from someone on the ground, and I continued to stand and watch the vision play out. Adrian scrambled to his feet, Tristan lying on the ground, bleeding from the stomach. Adrian dragged his wife out of the car before plunging the knife into her stomach repeatedly, then hopped in the car and drove off as fast as the tiny little engine could go.

My eyes followed the car until it was out of sight, and then fell on the clump of limps on the ground. The past-tense me had sat up, shoulder bleeding and neck injured, and cradled her dying husband in her arms. His intestines had been punctured and blood was pouring out of him fast. Even modern doctors wouldn't have been able to save the dying young man on the ground.

The wails coming from his wife's mouth were inhuman, and through her grief, she didn't see that Tristan had whispered his final words to her. The *"I love you"* fell on deaf ears, and his soul could not rest until he knew she heard his proclamation.

Cassandra was lying dead on the ground a few feet away; I had been the only one spared. For the second time in my life, I watch Tristan die. And for the second time in my life, I watch myself pick up the knife from the ground, and kill myself.

I feel the buzzing invade my body, and I know that it's time to return to the present. So, I close my eyes, and fall into blackness.

* * *

"Katherine? Katherine?" an unknown voice says, gently tapping my shoulder.

My eyes open, and I'm lying in an unknown room, with an unknown man leaning over me. I almost scream, until I see the stethoscope hanging around his neck.

"There she is. How are you feeling, young lady?" the older man asks.

It takes me a moment to remember all that happened, but when I do, I must give the doctor an answer, because he walks away. I'm in a hospital, which shocks me because Aunt Rachel told me that the closest hospital was nearly a half an hour away from our little ranch home. I'm expecting to have a panic attack in regards to what I just saw, but I don't. In fact, I feel as if another piece of the puzzle is being clipped in place.

"Sweetheart, you've got to drink more water during the day! You scared the living daylights out of me. Doc says you're dehydrated and overtired, so they'll keep you here tonight. You okay? You didn't bump your head or anything when you fell, did you?" Aunt Rachel asks, sitting in the chair beside my bed, taking my hand in hers.

I shake my head, suddenly drowsy. She must see this in my face because she walks across the room and flips the lights out. I smile in thanks, which I hope she can see even in the dull light. Spent, I barely finish praying before I drift into a sound sleep.

Chapter 12

I'm woken in the morning by a tugging on the back of my hand, and struggle to lift my heavy lids. The older doctor I vaguely remember from the night before smiles at me as he removes the IV from my hand.

"You sure do bruise easily, Miss. Prince. You'll have a nasty one on your hand from your IV, but no worries. You should feel good as new today," he says in a rumbling voice that belongs to a Santa Claus in the mall at Christmas time.

"Thanks, Doctor...?"

"Doctor Michael Colson," he says, shaking my hand lightly.

"I promise to drink more water," I say with a smile, knowing full well that dehydration had nothing to do with the reason I blacked out.

My aunt steps into the room from the hospital doorway, looking exhausted. I doubt she got any sleep last night in that lumpy chair and I feel a twinge of guilt for not insisting on leaving last night.

"Good morning, Katherine. Hope you're feelin' better. Doc says you should be rarin' to go and that everything's just fine," she says with a chipper tone that doesn't correspond with the bags under her tired eyes.

"Yeah, I feel great, actually," which isn't a lie.

"Tristan called your phone this morning when you didn't answer the door. I told him what happened and he said you felt faint yesterday after school and asked if it was alright he came over after classes today. I told him you'd be fine with it," she winks.

We leave the hospital and embark on the half an hour ride home in Aunt Rachel's newly fixed car. The first few minutes are filled with heavy silence, until we hit the highway and my aunt speaks.

"Katherine, you know your mother is the way she is for a reason, right?"

The random conversation starter throws me for a loop and I'm not sure what to say. My mother, who is supposed to be my best friend and guiding light, has been controlled and manipulated by my father, a man whose career as a police officer has hardened him. My mother had never stood up for me and never took the time to build any type of stable relationship with me, and the effects left me without paternal or maternal figures in my life.

"Yes, I know. Was she like this as a kid? So..." I can't even finish the sentence, but Rachel knows. She seems to know me inside and out.

"No, she wasn't. Not until she met your father. We don't have to talk about heavy stuff if you don't want to. In fact, I'll bet you're hungry. You'd think they'd feed you at that gosh darn place, but pudding and water just won't do," my aunt says, effectively ending our conversation. *Fine with me.*

We pull into a tiny diner called "The Beehive" that's straight out of the sixties. Once inside and seated, a preppy little waitress struts over to us, tucking a piece of her blonde hair behind her ear.

"What'll it be today?" she asks in an unpleasant voice. I have to cough to stifle a laugh; the girl is a walking Barbie.

"Two double bacon cheeseburgers with fries and chocolate milk shakes," says Aunt Rachel, not even giving me a chance to refute.

"Right up!" replies Barbie before gracefully waltzing away.

"Jeez, I think we just won 'spot the skank,' huh?" she whispers, making me laugh out loud.

"Tell me about you and Tristan. Two weeks isn't very long to have known a person, but you really seem to have taken a liking to him," my aunt says, genuinely interested.

I can't stop a smile from breaking across my face. "He and I are very similar. We like the same music, movies, sports, books, classes... he's a truly wonderful person."

Aunt Rachel smiles, flipping her blonde hair out of her eyes as she replies, "You know that he's had some rough patches, right? He isn't as squeaky clean as you'd like."

I shrug. "Neither am I," is all I say, which causes her to frown. "I'm not saying that to make you feel sorry for me, Aunt Rachel. I'm saying that because it's true, demons are hanging all over me, just waiting for a weak moment to pounce. I feel like, when I'm with Tristan, I'm stronger. I'm stronger because I have someone just like me, who knows my feelings inside and out. I'm not friends with him just for that reason; it's not like he's some weird rebound to help me stay afloat. He's genuinely a wonderful, pure of heart young man, and I would've been friends with him even if my life wasn't like it is now," I finish, my lengthy speech hanging in the air.

Aunt Rachel rests her chin on her fist, leaning on the table. "You're just friends? Maybe a lot has changed since my high school days, which weren't all that long ago, mind you, but it seems to me you don't go around holding hands with a friend. Or kissing said "friend," she raises her eyebrows.

My forehead scrunches, and a frown shows on my face. "We haven't really put a name to what we are. I don't think it matters much what we call our relationship; words are insignificant."

"So wise, Confucius. I'm impressed with your maturity, Katherine. Have I ever told you that? It's unfortunate; the circumstances under which you had to grow up so fast. But you're obviously where you need to be," she says, smiling a small, sad smile.

"Honestly, Aunt Rachel... I couldn't agree with you more," I say just as Barbie returns with our food.

We head back to the house holding our stomachs, overwhelmed from eating so much. It's nice to finally have an adult in my life; one that I can look up to. A woman like Aunt Rachel is the type of person everyone wants on their side: smart, witty, trustworthy and kind. How she's related to my mouse of a mother is a mystery to me, and why I've never tried to connect with my aunt before this year is puzzling. My mother and father always told me that she was an irresponsible partier that they didn't want brainwashing their children. If they thought that, why they would send me to stay with her is a mystery, too.

I think they knew she would break me out of my shell. They must have, because why else would they keep me from this amazing woman I've grown to love so much?

"Tristan gets out of school around noon, right?" my aunt asks, setting her backpack down.

"Yeah, he does."

"He'll probably be over soon. I think I'll head to the office, if you're feeling okay. Maybe you two should take a ride when he gets here, get some fresh air. Have you made any other friends? What about that nice girl who brought you home yesterday?"

"Sorren? Yeah, I feel close to her already; like I've known her for a while. It's kind of strange, actually. It's nice to have someone to just... be a girl with," I say, smiling to myself.

Suddenly, Aunt Rachel grabs my arm, tearing it away from my wrist where I was absently tracing my scars.

"Why do you always do that?" she says forcefully, surprising me with her venom.

My mouth pops open and I don't know how to answer. Why do I always trace my scars? Is it to remind myself of what I should never return to? Or am I punishing myself, my own form of punishment including having to look at the ugly mutilations on my wrists.

"I didn't know anyone noticed," is all I reply, unable to give her any other answer.

"Well I do. And I'd appreciate it if you'd stop," is all she says as she quietly walks out the door we just entered.

I stare at the wood, slightly warped and splattered with tiny white drips of paint, from an unfinished project, maybe. The house is deadly silent, filling the air with a thick feeling of loneliness that is all too familiar to me. For a few moments, I do nothing but breath in smells of cinnamon, lavender and vanilla; the smells of home.

I'm having one of those moments when you force yourself to stop and think about the mysteries of the world around you. When everything seems to be moving in slow motion but at warped speed at the same time. When you're afraid to think about the future, but forcing yourself to not think of the past. So what does that leave you to think of? Simply... the present.

A light knocking on the door disrupts my thoughts, and I am jarred from my moment by the sharpness of the sound. I open the door and find my angel himself. His eyes scan over me and I realize I probably look like death. I haven't showered or changed my clothes from yesterday and suddenly, I'm embarrassed. He must sense this because he speaks up.

"Are you feeling alright?" he asks, voice sounding casual but I can see the worry in his light blue eyes.

"Yes, I'm feeling fine. Nothing was actually wrong with me, Tristan. I had another... vision," I feel like an idiot saying that aloud, but there's no other word I can think of to describe what I saw.

His eyes grow wide, but before he has a chance to speak, I realize I haven't even brushed my teeth yet today. "Let me clean up, will you? I feel pretty scummy," I say.

"You're going to leave me in suspense?" he says, only half joking.

I laugh a little. "Sorry! Make yourself at home and I'll be out in a few minutes."

Leaving him in the living room, I saunter down the hall to the bathroom. I shower, shave, and towel dry my hair, which is magically straight today, and realize I forgot to grab clothes. I have my dirty ones that I wore before, but I refuse to put those back on because they smell like grease and hospital. Gross.

I wrap the towel around my torso and tie it in the front, fashioning a make-shift dress for the five foot walk to my bedroom. Hoping Tristan is on the couch, I open the door only to find him standing right in the middle of the hallway, looking at pictures on the wall. Steam from my shower made the wooden door stick and the popping sound it makes when I open it sends goose-bumps to my arms.

For a moment, we just stare at one another. His eyes automatically shift over my absurdly short towel-dress, but then he looks away with eyes that are embarrassed, lustful and ashamed.

"Well this is awkward," I say, laughing to myself as he makes a show of closing his eyes and shuffling down the hallway backwards.

Once in my room, I clothe myself in a pair of my favorite comfy jeans with a t-shirt that reads "Mount Amelia," the name of my old high school. The names of my former peers are listed on the back in two rows, with my "best friends" names circled with black sharpie, something Sam did at a sleepover during our freshman year. Only now do I realize that these girls, Sam and Julia, who were the only two people to ever *really* talk to me, were just using me for booze and invites to parties.

Thank God I'm a better judge of character now. Glancing in the dirty mirror on the wall, which could use some serious Windex, I apply the barest amount of mascara to my blonde eyelashes.

"Thanks. Sorry to keep you in suspense," I joke, but Tristan seems lost in his own little world. "Tristan? Anybody in there?" I ask, running my hand over his hair. My touch wakes him from his daydream, and he looks in my eyes with a concerned look on his face.

"Do you want to take Dino for a ride?" he asks, grabbing my hand while waiting for an answer.

I nod and smile. "I always thought having a 'spot' with your..." I cut myself off, not knowing how to finish the sentence. What I was going to say is, "*I always thought having a 'spot' with your boyfriend was cliché,*" but caught myself. I should ask him if he's my boyfriend. We've never officially discussed it.

He raises his eyebrows, waiting for me to finish, but I just shake my head, mumbling a "never mind." My answer obviously dissatisfies him, because he frowns.

The walk to the barn in a quiet one, but the silence isn't uncomfortable. His hand feels so strong, so sure, wrapped around mine that I forget all about the conversation we'll undoubtedly have once we get to the cliff. His thumb starts tracing little circles on the back of my hand, and I smile to myself, perfectly content.

"Hop on," Tristan says once we have Dino set to go. He waits for me to mount the black horse, then climbs on behind me, leading the horse on his way.

I'm shocked to find that the ride only takes ten minutes. "Hey, you knew there was a short cut?" I accuse.

His deep, throaty laughter sends bubbles into my stomach, more intense than butterflies. "Of course I knew there was a shortcut. Sometimes the long way is more fun," he says, resting his chin atop my head for a moment before dismounting the steed.

I cross my arms, trying to look angry, but the cute grin on his face makes it impossible not to smile back, but I roll my eyes anyway. He grabs my hand, helping my dismount, and Dino walks over to a patch of especially green grass before flopping down on his side with a thud.

"He's a strange animal," I say, but the horses head snaps up and our eyes connect as he huffs a snort, leading me to believe he heard me. "But a very smart one, yes," I say in a cooing voice while nodding my head, still looking at him. Tristan laughs, his whole body shaking and the sound reverberating off the trees.

We walk over to a patch of grass in direct sunlight, plopping down on the soft earth.

"So, how about you tell me what happened last night," he says, lying down on his back, stretching his arm out to the side, inviting me to do the same.

I lay next to him, our sides touching and his arm a soft pillow beneath my head. He smells like summer, somehow: sunshine, grass, and cinnamon that blend together to form a scent distinctly male. His body feels good, natural next to mine and I rest my head closer to his shoulder as I explain the vision.

Ten minutes later, Tristan's breaths have picked up speed and he's got that "I'm deep in thought" look on his beautiful face again.

"So? What do you think?" I ask when I can't take the silence anymore.

He sighs, using his free hand to rub his closed eyes. "Honestly Katie, I have no idea. And I don't think that any amount of thinking or hypothesizing is going to get us anywhere. If we're meant to find out, which we obviously are, we just have to wait for more clues. This is maddening. I can't believe it has to be you seeing these things! Why can't it be me? You've been through enough as it is," he says, sounding frustrated.

"Like you haven't?" I say, sitting up. "Don't doubt God; he knows what he's doing."

Tristan sits up too, looking at the sky. "I'll never doubt Him; I saw Him with my own eyes and have seen things that are unexplainable. I'm just aggravated that it has to be you." He touches my cheek, tucking my hair behind my ear. "I'm supposed to protect you. What if you get scared?"

I look at him sideways, taking a risk with my next words. "I don't need you to take every burden. Some things, by dealing with them, make you stronger. How do you think we are who we are right now?"

He looks away from me again, nodding. "Did you ever think that... you would ever heal this quickly?"

I know he doesn't mean physical healing, but rather the internal kind. "Not in a million years would I have ever thought it would be so... easy. I thought I'd have to deal with my Punishment for years, but He only punished me so I would know when I found you. Because you took them away. The emotions, that is."

And it's true; I never thought healing would be so simple. I've read books and seen movies where people spend years recovering from debilitating depression, but it only took me a few months. Granted my case is a spectacular one. Miraculous, even. It's shined a new light on my life like nothing ever has before. My heart was so mangled, so cracked and broken, that I thought the pieces would never click together again.

I trust God, but I thought he was angry with me for taking the life he gave me. Maybe I misread him entirely and he wasn't mad. Perhaps he has an ulterior motive.

"Tristan, have you dated a lot of girls?" the question literally pops out of my mouth before I think twice, the conversation with Malaya floods back into my mind.

He looks shocked, confused, and maybe a little embarrassed. "Uh, dated? No. I've never actually dated anyone," he says as he runs a hand through his light hair.

"Malaya cornered me in the hallway the other day and warned me about your womanizing tendencies. But you were only a sophomore, so how could you have dated the whole school? Unless you're some sort of 'super-player,' then I suppose that would explain things," I babble, a nasty tendency I have when I get nervous or feel threatened.

"Katie, I've never dated anyone. Have I been with girls before? Yeah, I have. Am I happy about it? No, I'm not. Would I ever do that again? Not for any amount of money in the world. Don't listen to Malaya; she's has the potential to be a nice girl, but she gossips like a grandma," he says, sounding too innocent.

Been with girls? Does that mean… "Wait, you're not a… virgin?" the shock seeps into my voice, along with hurt, which is irrational. Of course he had a life before me; I had one before him. Granted it was a rebellious one, much like his was, but I never went as far as sleeping with someone.

He takes a deep breath, obviously not happy with the change in conversation. "I am, but barely. Katie, you have to understand that I was a different person. For me to come back to this town after I was arrested, caught with drugs, found curled on my bathroom floor and sent to a psych ward..." he shakes his head. "For me to come back here is like the black plague hitting. But for me to come back an entirely different person than the guy this whole town knew me as?"

He covers his face with his hands for a moment before continuing. "That's like the apocalypse. Nobody knows what to think of me, or you, for that matter. But I think we shouldn't talk about this; the past. We were both different people now, and who we were? They don't matter anymore. If they *did,* we wouldn't be here. Literally, we would've died when we wanted to. Obviously we were brought back for a reason. But why us? What makes us so special? Thousands of people die every day, but *we* got second chances. *Us*, who everyone thinks are the most undeserving people of all! I suggest we focus on making it count."

He looks slightly winded after his lengthy speech, and I'll admit I'm pretty intimidated. The conviction in which he spoke is so strong that I feel it seeping into me and I feel a sudden urge to cry. Why *did* we get a second chance? Not to be self-deprecating, because I'm pretty proud of the person I'm becoming, but what's so special about me? It doesn't make any sense. There are suicide victims all over the world who don't come back.

"Why do I always seem to make you cry when I'm trying to do the opposite?" Tristan says, watching me from his position.

I didn't even realize the tears had slipped out, but now that I know that they have, I let them fall. He pulls me towards him and I climb into his lap, momentarily stunning him. His hands freeze in the air, but then caress my head, like a mother would a child. That somehow makes the tears fall faster, knowing I never had this as a child.

I feel the fluttering of his lips against my forehead, lighter than a moth's wing. The gesture makes me tip my head up in search for more, but when I go to press my lips against his, he leans away. This act of rejection burns through me like fire, sending a rock into the pit of my stomach and fresh tears to my eyes. I push him away, but he just grabs me again. I don't know why I'm crying anymore. I'm not this weak and I don't like the feeling of vulnerability.

"Katie," Tristan says as I try to quiet my breathing. "Katie, look at me," he says louder, grabbing my chin lightly in his hand, turning my head so he is looking me in the eye. "I'm not going to kiss you when you're upset. I don't want it to be a security gesture," he says, though I'm confused as to what he means.

After a few minutes, my pathetic blubbering simmers down and I lay back on the grass, hands folded together on my stomach, staring at the crystalline sky. There are no clouds anymore, and the sun is shining brightly. For a long while we just lay there, listening to one another's breaths and not thinking about anything in particular.

"You okay now?" Tristan asks with his voice steady and strong. Like always.

"Yes. Sorry," I say, completely embarrassed.

I don't need a boy to hold me when I cry; I'm just so used to doing it alone that I can't resist the arms of a friend. The word "friend" makes me want to scream with frustration, and my cheeks grow red remembering his rejection. A few more minutes pass and I watch the sunshine pass through the leaves of the trees, making a very natural and beautiful pattern on the ground.

"Katie?" Tristan asks, sounding unsure.

"What?" I say, not unkindly.

He shifts, moving into a sitting position, staring at me, like he's thinking. The wind blows, pushing up his hair and ruffling his button down shirt. He looks like a model, bathed in sunlight with eyes so blue that you think you're about to drown in the ocean. Without warning, he leans over me, his arm reaching across my body before resting his hand on the ground on the other side of me. He doesn't speak and neither do I, for this moment is so perfect I dare not disturb its flawlessness.

"If Malaya asks, will you tell her I'm your boyfriend?" he simply says, but shockingly, it doesn't break the spell. The beauty of his voice lulls me deeper into peace.

I nod and smile, knowing I *already* told her that. "If Scott asks, will you tell him I'm your girlfriend?" I reply, my voice sounding surprisingly sweet.

He smiles, moving closer, leaning over me until his head is blocking the sun. "The word is inaccurate, but it'll do. It's a hell of a lot less of an explanation," he winks.

By now, he's nose to nose with me, his eyes locking on mine with an intensity I've never seen before. The woods go silent and all I can hear is my heartbeat in my ears and my small intake of breath as his lips caress my cheek, just at the corner of my mouth. My eyes automatically close as he kisses my other cheek, his lips just barely touching mine.

I open my eyes for the briefest second to find him directly over me, but I snap them shut before I wake up from this dream. His lips hover over mine until I can't stand the separation anymore and I put an arm around his neck, pulling him to me. Our lips meet for the first time and bursts of white shine behind my closed eyelids.

I remember hearing a quote at some point in my life that went something like this: "It was not my lips you kissed, but my soul." I think Judy Garland said it, but whoever it was, thank you.

It feels like every word shared unshared is flowing between Tristan and I. It feels like every birthday wish I ever made, every dream I ever had, every beautiful thing I've seen or heard or tasted or felt is combined into this kiss. I always rolled my eyes at girls who thought they had found the love of their life in high school. Those girls who would kiss a boy and lose all common sense.

I am the world's biggest hypocrite and proud of it. I am "that girl" who *knows* she found the love of her life in high school; who just lost all common sense and every shred of doubt. This feels familiar, as though we've done it countless times before. My tongue caresses his lips and he sighs, so I grip him tighter, thinking he's about to pull away.

He isn't. He merely readjusts himself so that he lays closer to me, deepening our kiss in a way that is both innocent yet loving. I feel safe trapped in his arms, like nothing the world has to throw at me can hurt me. Most importantly, in his arms, I feel wanted. Like I'm finally worth something to someone and he isn't afraid to let me know that.

He can't know I'm in love with him; not yet. He would think I'm crazy, loving someone so deeply after only a short period of time. But this is what we're meant to do. We're meant to be with one another, regardless of circumstance and oblivious to time.

Time passes and the sun continues to move across the sky, casting shadows on the mountains. We lay there, wrapped in a bubble of happiness as his hand caresses my back from my neck to my tailbone. Surrounded by God's creatures, with the sounds of the earth wrapping us in a cocoon of serenity, he whispers my name.

And it has never sounded more beautiful.

● ●

Later that evening, Tristan helps me finish the massive amount of schoolwork I have accumulated after missing two whole days of classes. A text message from my aunt beeps in on my phone around six o'clock, telling me she's sorry but has to work late. I ask to invite Sorren over for dinner, but we really want to tell her about the vision I had the night before. She agrees, thankful to have an excuse to leave her house, and says she'll be over soon.

"You know this will drive her crazy, right? You really think we should tell her? What's she going to know that we don't?" Tristan asks, flipping the chicken breasts cooking in the oven.

I pause in stirring the lemon sauce for the chicken. "I think she has a right to know what's going on. I promised to keep her updated," I say, but Tristan's eyes fill with vexation.

"*We* don't even know what's going on yet. If she was supposed to know, don't you think she would've had a vision, too? She shared your first one," he says, shutting the oven door and clicking the timer on.

I cross my arms, feeling defensive. "So you're saying she doesn't deserve to know because she didn't see it? That means you don't deserve to know about either of these visions, Tristan. That isn't a valid argument."

He leans against the counter next to me, his shoulder level with my eyes. I look up, green meeting blue, and my defensiveness fades at the sadness in his weary eyes.

"I don't think we should scare her. We don't have an explanation for why you saw what you saw and if you tell her you witnessed her murder, she might be a bit... on edge, don't you think?" he says, making a very valid point.

I nod, looking at the bowl of lemon-flavored sauce on the counter. "Just you and me?"

"Against the world," he replies, intentionally making his statement corny. I snort and he can't help but join in a little bit, hoping to relieve the guilt and confliction I feel. "But yes, Katie. I think it makes the most sense to keep it between you and me."

He puts an arm around me and plants a kiss on the top of my head just as the front door springs open.

"Holy hell! Why is it that every second I see you guys, you're doing something mushy. Keep the gush-n-mush out of sight!" Sorren exclaims, shutting the door behind her before ripping off her Converse sneakers and throwing her keys in one of them.

She keeps her eyes away from mine as she walks into the hallway. Her posture sags and I notice she's limping slightly. Tristan and I exchange glances, both noticing the change in her demeanor. He removes his arm, a silent urging for me to go speak with Sorren.

The bathroom door is shut, but I knock on it and it opens. I watch as Sorren quickly readjusts her pant leg, which she had hiked up to her knee. Our eyes connect and I see pain and worry in her dark brown eyes, which are bloodshot. I shut the bathroom door behind me before facing her. I know the signs; I *had* the signs not too long ago.

"Your mom or your dad?" I ask, gesturing to her leg, which she holds slightly off the ground.

She hangs her head, brushing a hand over her forehead. "I figured you knew. You've got that *look* all over you," she says, sitting on the closed toilet seat.

"What look? My aunt doesn't hurt me," I say, confused.

Sorren scoffs, rolling her eyes. "Oh please, don't play dumb with me, princess."

I hold my hands up and raise my eyebrows, a confused look no doubt gracing my face.

"That chariness to your eyes. That suspicious, guarded look you think nobody notices? I can spot it a mile away. The only time I don't see it is when you're with *him*," she nods her head towards the door.

"Sorren, I can help you. I went through it and look where I am now. You can be different; you can change things. Does anybody know?"

She sighs, slowly propping her foot against the bathtub across from her. "You do. I think Malaya does."

"Malaya?" I question, shocked.

"She's not a bad person. She makes stupid mistakes and follows the crowd, but she's a nice girl. Tristan screwed her over, so she harbors some serious misplaced hatred."

Sorren looks like she's expecting me to question her about Malaya and Tristan's falling out, but to her dismay, I stick to the problem at hand. "Don't try to switch the topic. I know all the tricks, alright?"

She looks at me, anger churning behind her expression. "This isn't a regular thing. My mom drinks a lot and loses her head sometimes. Back off, 'kay Dr. Phil?"

I roll my eyes, but really I just want to hug her. "Then what were the marks around your neck yesterday? And where are they today?" I ask, noticing her un-bruised neck.

"You really want to know?" she asks, skeptical. "If I told you they didn't come from my mother, would you just believe me and not ask me to elaborate?"

I've known the girl for two days. Yes, I feel like I've known her forever, but do I really expect her to trust me? No. Because girls like us-her- do anything they can to keep from letting people know. I'll bet her heart is racing and her palms are sweating right now, just thinking about what might happen if I tell an adult about her mom. The fear. The hopelessness. The terror.

"I'd trust you, but now I'm curious."

She crosses her arms, looking me straight in the eye. "This guy I was with got a little rough. I wasn't complaining," she states, matter of fact.

I'm sure my face went fifty shades of red before settling on the light rose it is now, but I try to look like I don't care. "You can't let this kind of stuff happen to you, Sorren. There are people who can help you."

"What kind of stuff? Rough sex?" she asks, laughing. "Look, Kath, just leave me alone about it, okay? My mom got pissed because I mouthed off. This kind of thing doesn't happen all the time. I'm fine."

I don't believe her for a second. Before, she made it sound like this was an everyday thing, now she's recanting that statement? To appease her, I shrug and turn around, opening the door.

"Hey, Kath?" she asks, voice meeker, more vulnerable, and lacking its usual spunk.

"Yeah?" I say, hopeful she'll confide in me.

"Can I stay here tonight?" she asks, playing with her hands on her lap, avoiding my gaze.

Sadness grips my heart at the frailty of her voice, but I reply with a smile and tell her yes. Walking down the hallway, I close my eyes and force the flashbacks away, chanting in my head that *I'm alright, I'm alright, I'm alright...*

"She okay?" Tristan asks, pulling the chicken out of the oven with a pink, frilly dish towel.

I sigh, shaking my head. The bathroom door creaks open and all I say is, "I'll tell you another time. She's okay, for now."

His brow furrows, marring his heavenly face with worry, but he nods. He plates dinner, drizzling the sauce over the chicken and tossing some salad from the garden into bowls. There's more than enough for the three of us, so we leave the remaining food on the counter for when my aunt gets home.

"So, shall we play a game?" asks Sorren, wiggling her eyebrows up and down as she shovels a piece of the delicious chicken into her mouth.

Tristan finishes chewing and then asks, "What type of game?"

"A truth game. Something to help us catch up from two-plus years without each other," says Sorren, bringing back the awkwardness that had faded a few minutes ago.

Tristan flashes me a grin, his white teeth peeking from behind his perfect lips. Lips that I kissed today. A smile slowly grows on my face, accompanying the memory.

"Katie and I've already played this game. It wouldn't be much fun, playing with us," says Tristan, still looking at me.

Sorren dramatically sighs, drawing my attention from Tristan. "You guys are no fun. Got any booze?" she perks up, looking excited.

My eyebrows shoot up, surprised at her request. "Sorren, it's a school night! You really want to show up to school trashed?"

"Speaking of school, why weren't you there today?" she asks, changing the subject so quickly I feel like I just got whiplash.

"I wasn't feeling well. Probably because I passed out yesterday," I say, spearing a piece of chicken on my fork and plopping it in my mouth, feeling the sweet juices spread across my tongue.

"Yeah, that was weird. You feeling better now, at least? Have any new-slash-important freaky visions I should know about?" she asks, speaking with her mouth full of salad.

Years of lying are coming in handy at this moment. I know exactly how to lie; I'm somewhat of an expert. It doesn't feel good, lying to this girl I so obviously share some type of divine connection with, but it's a necessity.

"Nothing," I say, voice perfectly even. Sorren doesn't notice a thing and the look in Tristan's eyes tells me that he's impressed and worried about how well I fib. I put my hand on his knee under the table, making him smile to himself. Across from us, Sorren makes an exaggerated gagging sound, which pisses me off but I manage to ignore it.

We spend the rest of the evening enjoying the meal Tristan and I cooked together. It's nice to feel like I belong; there's a peace in my heart that I've never felt before. I'm having one of those philosophical moments where I think about how my life has changed and how blessed I am. The peace is shattered with the annoying ringing of the home phone, which is strange because I only ever hear it ring when Rachel's boyfriend calls.

"You gonna get that?" Tristan asks, seeing the deliberation on my face.

I nod a little too forcefully and stand from the chair, which makes a screeching noise as it slides across the wooden floor. The incessant ringing makes the hair on my arms stand up, and I don't know why.

"Hello?" I say, sounding more irritated than I would like to.

There's shuffling and rapping noises coming through the line but no voices. Eeriness fills the air when the sounds halt, silence pouring from the other end of the call.

"Hello?" I repeat, sounding more afraid than I wished.

I feel like I've been tossed into one of those horror movies when the killer is on the phone, silently listening to his next victim panic. I hastily hang up the phone, but I can't stop the feeling of dread that seeps through me. It starts off slow, but I feel an instinctive need to double check that the doors and windows are locked.

A pair of hands lands on my shoulders, making me jump and release a small screech. I whirl around only to find a set of crystal blue eyes widening in shock at my outburst. I'm being silly... prank phone calls happen all the time. There's no need to have a panic attack over someone calling the wrong number.

"Sorry. That kind of freaked me out, that's all. Someone had the wrong number, I guess," I say, breathless and embarrassed by my reaction.

"Unless it's Jack the Ripper's zombie, rising from the grave to attack the-" Sorren says, but is interrupted by Tristan.

"Shut up, Sorren. That's not funny," he says, voice dropping a few tones in seriousness.

Sorren slams her palm on the table and stands dramatically. "Jesus, Tristan! When did you become her freakin' body guard? I was just joking, okay? Lighten up and stop being an asshole," she yells.

An extraordinarily uncomfortable silence fills the room and I wish I was being consumed by quick-sand or taken away by an extra-large bird... Anything to escape this seriously awkward moment.

"You're so insensitive! Can you not tell when someone's upset? All you think about is yourself! That hasn't changed one bit!" Tristan says and the venom in his voice shocks me.

"*I'm* insensitive?! Where were you for the past two and a half years, Tristan? When I needed you, where were you?"

"Are you calling me selfish? Do you seriously think I was in any position to help *you*? You completely deserted me when Sky died, and you know it," raw emotion seeps into his voice, causing it to shake.

Sorren's eyes fill with tears that don't spill over, but glisten in her eyes like dew on a rose petal. "How was *I* supposed to know how to help you? Do you not remember the things you did before they sent you away? Do you not remember who you became?"

"I sent you a letter the moment I arrived at John Adam's. I had already changed, Sorren. You didn't even let me tell you that," Tristan says.

I want to sink into the floor. The tension between the two of them has been growing since the moment Sorren walked in the door tonight, but I wasn't anticipating being present when they hashed it out.

"A person doesn't change in a week, Tristan. You're claiming you turned your life around in one week? You were a mess! You felt *nothing*! You were a shell. The only emotion you ever showed at all was hatred, and even that was weak at best. You can't just wake up one morning and shout 'Hallelujah' to the heavens and be healed! That's impossible, and you're an idiot if you believe that."

That sparks a thought in me; is that when Tristan's punishment started? Even before he tried killing himself? I wonder what God's plan is. What the purpose of all this was. Surely there's a reason things happened the way they did. I don't have time to ponder these new thoughts, because I hear my name spewed from Sorren's mouth.

"If you've changed as much as you claim to have, as much as you're fooling everyone into believing, then why do you spend every waking moment with her?" I'm shocked to hear her vituperation continue. "She's not me, Tristan. What happened to me? You didn't even tell me you were back in town!"

By now, Sorren's face is red and portrays a wide range of emotions. I'm not sure whether anger, frustration, sadness or confusion sent her over the edge, but maybe it's a combination of them all. I know what it's like to feel things amplified, and I am unable to be angry at her for bringing me into this conversation.

"Don't bring Katie into this, Sorena! This is about you and me, not me and Katie. What we do is none of your business," Tristan says, trying to diffuse the situation but failing miserably.

Sorren scoffs and continues. "You were always my business. You've known her, what... a month? At most? That's pathetic! You've known me since birth and you've never looked at me the way you look at her."

A tiny crinkle forms in Tristan's forehead, one I've only seen a handful of times when he's thinking particularly hard about something. I back away a little, looking to give them more space, but it seems like they've both forgotten I am here.

"Are you serious? You're really going there?" Tristan asks, sounding annoyed.

"Of course! You agreed to give it a try, Tristan!" Sorren exclaims, stepping from around the table to stand right in front of the red-faced blonde haired boy.

"We were sixteen! I'm not the same person you thought you loved. Real love doesn't exist when you're fifteen and sixteen years old, Sorren!"

Another piece of the puzzle clicks together and my mouth pops open. In the moments I've heard Sorren talk about Tristan, she's always used a softer, sweeter tone than she usually speaks in. When she laid her hand on his arm until he pulled away. When she couldn't even look at him in the parking lot. When she just complained about us being too affectionate in her presence.

Sorren is in love with Tristan. But not my Tristan; not the good, nurturing, soul-mate Tristan God sent just for me. She loves the boy she thought she knew. The boy who thought he knew himself until tragedy struck and he lost everything he once had. The boy she claims was never there for her.

"It doesn't matter what you think! I refuse to just sit here and act like this," she gestures to me and back to Tristan, "doesn't bother me! I've waited for you to come back to me for two years, hoping you had found yourself again! And now that you have, you don't even have the decency to set me straight?"

Tristan steps away from an approaching Sorren who looks like she's about to smack him. "You want me to set you straight?" Sorren nods. "Okay then. I'll just say it then. I'm in love with Katie. I've known her for two years. She and I shared letters; letters that helped me heal and become who I am now. So you cannot tell me that I don't know her like I know you. It takes a special type of person to bring someone out from the dark, and Katie did that for me when you weren't here to do it."

Sorren slaps Tristan in the face before theatrically departing from the room. A moment later, the front door slams with enough force to shake the kitchen floor. We remain silent for a moment, both at a loss of words. I might have just lost the only friend I really made here; my ally and the person I have a strange connection with. Something in my heart tells me that things will work out for the best and not to fret, but the sting of her words sends bolts of sadness to my chest.

Arms wrap around me, comforting me in their embrace. Our breaths are in sync and his body presses mine against the counter. I don't pull apart; I just stand there with my hands trapped against his chest and ear pressed to his heart- *my* heart- beating in the silence.

"I'm sorry," is all he says.

He shouldn't feel bad, and none of this is his fault, but the words help me relax. We do nothing; only hold each other until a crack of thunder shakes the house. Rain starts pounding on the roof in rhythmic taps, adding a very natural soundtrack to the atmosphere. Tristan and I end up curled on the couch as the sounds of thunder and rain lull us into sleep.

I awake gasping, shaking from head to toe with the sound of my scream echoing off the walls. It takes me a moment to come back to reality, but when I see the comforting walls of my bedroom, I take a calming breath. I remember falling asleep on the couch, so Tristan must have carried me to bed. A knock on my door makes me jump.

"Hi, baby. You okay?" my aunt asks, wearing her sleep clothes and glasses. She looks exhausted.

My heart still pounds and my throat is so dry I can't speak, but I nod. I don't even remember what the dream was about, but it terrified me. My aunt leaves the doorway but the kitchen light flicks on seconds later and the sound of the water running makes me lick my dry lips.

"Here you go," says Rachel's sweet voice as she sits on my bed.

I feel like a child, but the sensation is new. The feeling of being loved and looked after and protected is foreign to me, and warmth drives away my terror. My aunt strokes my hair, calming me with her mere presence. I look at the scene in the mirror across from my bed, feeling like I'm watching a film. This is what a mother should do. This is who a mother should be. It makes me sad knowing that women like my Aunt Rachel don't have children but people like my parents do. My parents, who are so deranged they don't even deserve the title.

"Why don't you have kids?" I ask, breathless from gulping my water.

She smiles a sad smile that adds years to her youthful face. "I can't. I'm sterile. But there're plenty of kids out there who could use someone to love them, and I'd happily oblige. Just because I didn't birth them doesn't mean I can't love them the same way I would love my own child," she says, kissing my forehead.

I wonder if I should be embarrassed; I'm a senior in high school for goodness sakes! I shouldn't enjoy being babied by my aunt. However, I've never been one for traditional beliefs, and I soak up her attention like a sponge.

"Is there anything you want to talk about?" she asks, getting more comfortable on my bed.

"Did you know? About my father?" I ask, darkness creeping into my voice with every word.

She looks confused. "You've gotta be a little more specific than that, sweetie."

"Did you know he hurt us?" I clarify, speaking for my mother, brother and myself.

A clouded look enters her eyes at my question and I get the distinct feeling that she doesn't want to answer. "Not until your mom sent you here."

Confusion must be splashed across my face because my aunt elaborates. "You really think your mom wanted to send you away? That she didn't think she could help you more than I can?"

"Then why did she send David away?" I ask, still slightly unsure.

"David needs help, honey. He isn't going to heal by himself. Your mom told me that from the moment you woke up in that hospital after your... accident, that there was a light in your eyes that only came with sanity and understanding. She said you finally *felt* again; that you showed emotions again. Your brother is not in a good place right now, Katherine. He needs professional help."

My mother sent me here to protect me. The thought makes tears spring to my eyes, but I hold them back. I am so fed up with this crying business.

"It's okay to cry, Katie. No one is expecting you to be strong all the time."

I clench my teeth and force the tears back, refusing to let things I can't change break me. There's no use dwelling over the bad. The point of life is to make the best of things and to do what God expects us to do: help others, try to forgive, and be the best we can be. However, my heart is still to broken to fully forgive. I know that, with God's guiding hand, I can eventually become the full, complete person he said I will be. But for now, my heart is still mending. For now, there are still missing pieces.

Chapter 13

The next morning, I awake to a breeze blowing across my face. It's chilly enough to raise goose-bumps on my skin and all I want to do is burrow deeper under the covers. A hand gently touches my shoulder and I would have been terrified had I not recognized the feeling that accompanies Tristan whenever he comes near me.

"Good morning, beautiful. I heard you had a rough night. It's earlier than usual, but why don't you get up and we'll go get coffee?" he asks in a sweet voice that reminds me of how he speaks to Dino. I smile.

He moves in to kiss me, making me move away. His face is so shocked I can't help but release a tiny giggle. I want to brush my teeth before he kisses me. Wouldn't want to scare him away.

"You've got thirty minutes before I drag you to my truck, ready or not!" he calls as he walks out of the room. Rachel must already be gone for work; her schedule is so unpredictable.

I decided to shower, thinking the hot water would help me relax my nerves, which are on edge thanks to the revelations from the night before. The water works wonders on my skin, which was pale when I woke up but is now a healthy looking rose color. My eyes look especially green today, so I apply some mascara to intensify their already bright color. It isn't often my eyes are this shade of green, so I intend to make the most of it.

"How much time do I have before you kidnap me?" I yell through the house jokingly, pulling on underwear and snapping my bra. I completely forgot to close my bedroom door.

"Katie, are you *trying* to kill me?" I hear an exasperated voice say from the hallway and I turn around to see him retreating down the hall. "Close your door next time!"

I laugh, hard, but feel a little insulted. He is my boyfriend... doesn't he *want* to see me this way? "It's my house! I can prance around totally naked if I felt like it," I reply, still laughing to myself.

I hear a groan, followed by what sounds like the knocking of a head on the cupboards in the kitchen. "Katherine! You're seriously testing my will-power," he calls back.

Not five minutes later I enter the kitchen, wet hair piled on top of my head and uniform in place. I walk right up to Tristan and grab his hands in my own, standing several inches away, only our hands touching. His eyes move over mine, like he's seeing into the depths of my very essence. It's a frightening feeling, really... to be so totally connected and enthralled in a person.

People would probably ask me why I don't bother getting closer to others. If I had told them the truth, that I feel like I have all I'll ever need and all I'll ever want in Tristan, they'd call me a co-dependent girlfriend on the road to a teen pregnancy and heartbreak. But if they knew our story, our connection... if they felt a fraction of what I felt for the angel standing before me, they'd understand.

When God gives you all you'll ever need, there's no reason to go searching for something else. I've made "friends" at school; people you say hello to in the hallways and smile at and laugh with at moments. I use the word friend loosely because I think people need to earn the title. For now, they are merely friendly acquaintances.

"What are you thinking about?" he asks, brow furrowed.

I smile and shake my head, not wanting to put my feelings into words. "Let's go!" I say, tugging on his hands and out the door. The day is overcast but still bright, so I fish my sunglasses out of my backpack as Tristan opens my door.

"You seem rather chipper for someone who I was told had a rough night," he says, sliding behind the wheel of his pick-up.

"I'm not, really. I'm just embracing a new motto I claimed last night. I'll explain it to you another time, though. Let's just try to forget last night happened," I say. Avoidance is not a ticket to happiness, but it's all I have at the moment.

We arrive at a little coffee shop not far from the school and I take a seat as Tristan goes to order us two iced cappuccinos.

The tiny café has elevator-music playing, which is irritating... why does everything have to be so bland and unoriginal? A bell dings, signaling someone has entered the shop.

"Hey, Katherine!" says an annoyingly cocky voice from behind me.

Turning, I see Scott walking towards my table for two. He's either oblivious to the fact that I'm here with Tristan and doesn't even notice him standing twenty feet away, or just doesn't care.

"Thanks for saving me a seat," he winks. But it doesn't even look like the smooth, debonair gesture he was aiming for; it looks like a twitch. I stifle a laugh by coughing, but it doesn't sound convincing, even to my own ears.

"I'm here with-" I begin, but a *genuinely* debonair boy cuts me off.

"Her boyfriend," Tristan says, sounding pleased and not unkind.

"Hey, Trist. Congrats, man," Scott says awkwardly, but he doesn't stand. Instead, he says, "Pull up a chair! Party of three," which makes me snort playfully. Tristan can't help but smile.

"How've you been, T? I haven't… really… talked to you since you, uh, came… home," Scott says, and I'm somewhat surprised to hear true concern and regret in his choppy sentence.

"I'm great now, Persico. Found what I needed," Tristan replies, sipping his iced coffee and passing me mine as he drags a nearby chair over to the small, crowded table.

"Well, I should get going. Don't want to be late, right? Later, T," Scott says, squeezing Tristan's shoulders, which makes him cringe ever so slightly. "Later, Katherine!" he twitches again, this time deliberately making a fool out of himself.

The bell dings again; Scott didn't even get a coffee. "That was weird," I say, trying to make light of an uncomfortable situation.

"He's an idiot but he was always a good friend. You find out who your real friends are after tragedy strikes, because they'll still stick by you. I guess I didn't have any real friends," he says bitterly, which makes my mending heart ache.

My hand reaches across the tiny table and grasps his, which is so much larger than mine it's comical. The feel of his skin on mine is comforting and as I rub tiny circles onto his palm, I don't know what I'd do without him.

"I don't know what I'd do without you," I say, feeling a heaviness in my chest thinking of how I felt before I almost took my own life. So full of bitterness and hatred that I stopped believing in the good things around me.

He just smiles, which is nice because we don't need words. Here, in this tiny little coffee shop that smells like burned toast and espresso, another piece of my heart clicks into place. It's a feeling like no other and I can't anticipate when it's going to happen, but I love the feeling it brings. A peace settles over me, warming my skin and making the world a little brighter. I have a feeling Tristan knows exactly what's happening to me, because his face takes on a softness that contrasts his rugged looks.

"Come on. Let's get to school, shall we?" I say, standing up and tucking my arm through his.

■■

When we get to school Tristan shucks his leather jacket and tosses it in the almost non-existent backseat. His strong jawline and somewhat shaggy hair look silly attached to a body dressed in a preppy looking school uniform. I lean over and plant a kiss on his jaw, but he moves so I end up kissing his neck instead. A sexy half-smile graces his face as he unlocks and opens his door to get out.

"So what do you think Sorren will have to say today?" he asks, taking my hand as we pass a group of rowdy boys throwing a football back and forth. Some of them smile at me and I offer tiny waves to the girls sitting on the grass.

"Hey, Katie! Hey Tristan!" shouts Alexis, the girl in my AP Spanish class who I've helped with her homework. We both wave and Alexis' friends Ellen and Justine shout their greetings.

"Is it strange how things... completely turned around?" I say as another girl, one of Malaya's friends, says hi to me.

Tristan releases my hand only to wrap an arm around my shoulders and caress my cheek. "Katie, I don't think you know how much people like you. You don't even have to talk to them on a daily basis; they just genuinely like you. They tolerate me because they're afraid I'll go postal," he jokes, but I bet he's actually being completely serious.

I roll my eyes, but a bit of well-deserved pride wells up inside of me. People like me; for who I am. People I've never shared my past with, who aren't looking at me like I'm a kicked puppy in need of rescuing. It's nice to know you're liked for *you*.

"You know, it must be a sin to be so... content. Something's bound to happen that knocks everything to the ground," says Tristan, rubbing my shoulder with his tan hand.

My mouth falls into a frown, not taking any comfort at all in his words. I shrug them off as we enter the halls of the school just as the first bell rings.

••

Later than night, Tristan is in the kitchen with me. Sorren never showed up at school today and her car was missing from her driveway, so we have no idea where she could possibly be. What a coward; to completely skip school because of a fight between your friends? Worst things could happen, she has no idea.

"Do you think you could do me a favor, Tristan?" I ask, rubbing my forehead with my hand.

"Of course. What's up?" he says, closing the refrigerator and walking towards me.

"Could you run to the store and get me some Tylenol? I have a wicked headache," I say, hating that I have to ask him. I've always hated taking things from people, even favors. Actually, especially those.

"Yeah, I'll go right now. Anything else?" he asks, shrugging on his leather jacket and twirling his keys.

"No. Thanks," I say, genuinely glad I don't have to go without some type of pain medicine tonight.

"Anything for you, angel," he winks, but it's cute, unlike Scott's twitch. He kisses me on the forehead and gently strokes my hair for a moment before walking away.

When I hear the front door close, I stand. My vision swirls and black dots dance across my eyes. The phone rings, sending a sharp pain to my head. I lumber across the kitchen and rip it off the hook, nearly slamming it to my ear in frustration.

"Hello?" I say, sounding annoyed.

"Is this Ms. Rachel Sullivan?"

The use of my aunt's last name disarms me; I very rarely hear my mother's maiden name spoken aloud. My father forbade it.

"No, she isn't home. Who's calling?" I say, trying to appear friendlier.

"Is this Miss. Katherine Prince?" he asks, a sense of urgency slipping into his voice.

"Who's calling?" I ask again.

"Katherine, this is Detective Hayes from the Los Angeles Police Department. Are you home alone?"

This is weird. Who do I know in Los Angeles? How do I know this man is a real cop? Well... he knows my name and Rachel's name, and that I'm staying with her. There's a sign.

"Yes, Sir," my voice sounds so hesitant that he picks up immediately.

"Katherine I need you to do me a favor. Lock all your windows and doors and turn off all the lights. Do that now, but stay on the phone with me," he says using a tone that sets me on edge.

"Why?" I say, confused.

"Just do as I say, Katherine. But stay on the phone," he urges.

My heartbeat picks up but something inside me tells me to listen to the mysterious man on the other side of the phone. "I have to put the phone down; it's not cordless," I say, voice shaking.

"Do that. Lock everything in the house and turn off all the lights. Where are you right now?" he asks, still sounding tightly controlled. Robotic.

"The kitchen."

"Are there any other phones in the house?"

I shake my head, but feel stupid because he obviously can't see me. "No. I'll go do as you say."

So I do. I lock every window and every door and turn off all the lights. My heart is pounding so fast that my hands start sweating and I almost drop the phone when I get back into the kitchen.

"I did it, I did what you said. What's going on? What's wrong?" I say, starting to get really afraid. If this is some type of prank call, I'm going to murder the perpetrator.

"Where is your Aunt, Katherine?"

"Stop asking me questions and answer mine! What the hell is going on!?" I shout, the loudness of it filling the frighteningly empty house.

"I'm not sure how aware you are of the murders that have been committed in the Los Angeles area in the past few days?" he says, and I'm happy we're making some progress here.

"No, I have no idea what murders you're talking about. They haven't been in the news. What do they have to do with me?"

"Please keep your voice down, Katherine, merely as a precaution. Your brother has been identified as the killer, Miss. Prince. Your father was found dead in your home last night around seven in the evening. I am so very sorry, Katherine," he says, his robotic voice tapering off.

My heart stops beating. The world seems to freeze around me: the clock stops ticking, the wind stops blowing, the rain stops beating against the roof. The only sound I hear is my own heartbeat and breaths, escalating towards hyperventilation.

"Katherine? Katherine, I need you to listen to me, sweetheart. I know this is hard but you need to keep calm. We've contacted your local police and they're calling in reinforcements from the other local departments."

"Reinforcements? What makes you think he'd come here?" I stammer out, momentarily regaining control of my senses. *Stay calm, stay calm, stay calm, Katie,* I chant in my head

"He called this phone number last night from your home. Did you receive any mysterious calls?"

A sob escapes my mouth, but I squelch it with my free hand. Tears begin to roll down my face, but I stay strong. I need more information. I need facts to keep me weighted, because if I let myself think and speculate, I'll break. I won't just break, I'll shatter.

"It's okay, Katherine. We'll keep you safe. We had no cause to believe he would go to your residence until we checked phone records today. There was a clerical error; we were unaware of his calling your aunt's home."

The silence is deafening. My heartbeat breaks the quiet with its loud bumps, but I feel empty, like my heart is nowhere to be found. I hate this feeling, so I say a quick prayer. I feel the Holy Spirit fill me with reassurance that the Lord is with me. The feeling makes me stronger.

"How many people...?" I can't finish the sentence.

"At least six. We don't know all the details yet, but your mother is safe and sound. Your father was found dead this morning and your mother locked in an upstairs closet," the Detective says, sounding rehearsed but genuine.

Another sob escapes me and I crouch on the floor of the kitchen, clutching the phone as a crack of lightning lights up the room. The rain halts suddenly and everything is still.

He locked her in the same closet our father locked us in when he would beat our mother. We would be in there for hours, listening to the sounds of skin on skin and screaming words about food, cleanliness, ignorance and self-worth. David and I used to clutch each other and huddle on the floor, humming to try to drown out the sounds. It was horrifying. Actually, I used to clutch David. He would just stare at the wall, motionless as a stone, scolding me for humming.

Suddenly, the roaring of Tristan's truck returns and my stomach drops to the floor. I gasp, stunned and feeling guilty I forgot I sent him to the store for me.

"Oh my gosh!" I exclaim, nearly dropping the phone in my haste to get up. "My boyfriend, he's outside! I forgot I sent him to the store! He needs to come inside!"

"No! Katherine, don't leave-" I don't listen to the rest of his words, but instead drop the phone and race through the kitchen to the living room. I tear open the front door just as Tristan is climbing out of his truck. A feeling of pure terror courses through me at the feeling that we are not alone. Despite my earlier conviction and the Detective's orders, I panic.

"Tristan! Get inside!" I scream, bounding down the steps, wanting to yank him into the house with my own two hands. His handsome face is shocked before turning ash white. He sways and falls back against his truck before connecting his frightened eyes with mine.

"Hey, sis," a gravelly voice whispers a few inches from my ear as an arm wraps itself around my neck.

Chapter 14

Tristan

Of course I get the slowest store clerk in town. Her nametag says Melissa, but it looks half-scribbled out with Sharpie.

"Evening," I greet when I finally get in front of her.

Wordlessly, she scans the bottle of Tylenol and drops it into the plastic bag with a blank expression.

"Thanks," I say, shoving my change in my jacket pocket and high-tailing it out of the 24-hour mini-mart.

The storm has picked up, making the trees bow like fans at a rock concert. The allusion makes me smile a little as I jog to my truck. I try to use as little gas as possible, because Rachel so graciously pays for it without even a second glance. I'm not sure how aware Katie is of her aunt's financial situation, but the woman is richer than God. Not literally, of course, but no other metaphor explains the amount of her wealth in such detail. The woman could buy half the state if she was of mind to.

That's what I love about Rachel, her kindness and utter humility. Nobody even knows about the couple million bucks she has saved in the bank from a lottery win a few years back, and I'm certainly not going to spill her secret.

The ride home is uneventful, but the rain suddenly stops as I turn onto Katie's isolated street. It's pitch black outside because the moon is hiding behind the thick storm clouds that have been haunting us all day. A horrible feeling washes over me, like I shouldn't be here. The unease intensifies when Rachel's house comes into view and it's barely visible because all the lights are off. When I left not a half an hour ago, the majority of the lights were on. Katie hates the darkness.

My truck rolls up the rocky driveway and the uneasy feeling makes my heart pound, and I swear I feel Katie's heart beating right alongside mine. Something isn't right...

I leave the headlights on so I can find my way to the door. The rusty door of my pick-up pops open, breaking the eerie silence with its sound. Katie opens the door of her house, looking unlike anything I've ever seen before. Her clothes are slightly rumpled and her hair is out of the tight bun it's been in all day, so her waves are bouncing down past her elbows. But it's not her body language that scares me; it's her eyes.

Those beautiful green eyes I see reflected in the dim light of my truck's headlights are filled with a terror so thick that it makes me physically stumble backwards a step, making me hit my back against the truck's side. A shadow passes behind her and a face I will never forget protrudes from the darkness and bathes itself in the light from my headlights.

"Tristan! Get inside!" Katie screeches as she jumps down the steps, arms slightly extended like she wants to pick me up. She must know. She must have known he was out here and she still came for me. To warn me? To protect me? How foolish. It's *my* job to protect *her*.

"Hey, sis," David's voice sounds dry, like he hasn't had a drip of water in days. His hair is long, resting on his shoulders, and darker than I remember it being. But I don't have time to focus on his appearance because his arm wraps itself around my angel's neck.

She screams and tries to throw him off, but his other hand comes up to her face, gently stroking it with his knuckles. The gesture would've been comforting had it not been for the giant knife he held in his fist. Its long blade glinted in the light, the glare hitting me in the eyes for a moment. Katie stops squirming and closes her eyes. She's praying, I know she is. I can feel it in the air, the Lord's presence.

"Well, well, well, sissy! You got yourself a nice little house here. You'll be so happy when you hear what I've done for us. I saved us! I saved you! You're safe now, sissy! He's gone!" David says, turning Katie around so that she's no longer facing me. His hands rest on her shoulders possessively and I can't tear my eyes away from the knife in his hand, inches from her precious neck.

"David, please don't hurt me," she says, sounding shockingly calm. I'm proud of her bravery for a moment, until the terror kicks in a millisecond later.

"Hurt you? I'd never hurt you, sissy! I've missed you," he pulls her close, inhaling the scent of her hair and rocking her back and forth. She's stiff as a board, not moving, barely breathing.

"Dave. Why don't you let her go and we can go inside and you can tell us everything you did for Katie," I say, unable to stay quiet a moment longer. I can't watch him hold her; can't stand the sight of his hands on her beautiful body.

He freezes and stops rocking her, gaze snapping up and gray eyes meeting mine before narrowing into slits. "Who are you?" he says, pulling Katie closer, closer to him and to the blade in his hand. I gulp.

"I'm Katie's best friend. I've heard... a lot about you. She isn't feeling well so why don't you let her go lay down and you and I can talk while she's resting?" I say, playing along. It's what I've seen nurses do at John Adam's when patients were being particularly hard to deal with.

"You want her to leave me? After I just found her again?" he laughs, an insane sounding one that sends prickles to the surface of my already freezing skin. "You're not taking her from me!"

Katie makes eye contact with me, silently pleading with me to leave. I can see it in her eyes that she wants me to just hop back in my truck and speed off. Not a chance.

"I don't want to take her from you. She just isn't feeling very well. I picked her up some medicine so we should let her lay down, Dave," I say.

He takes a few steps back and I instinctively take a step towards him, which he notices. "Stop it! Don't make me hurt her. I don't want to hurt her," he says, whirling Katie around so that she's facing me again. He moves the knife so that the tip barely rests on her stomach, but each time she breathes, her delicate skin presses into it a little more. My blood starts to boil and anger replaces a bit of the terror.

"Dave, let her go. Tell me about everything you did for her. I want to make her as happy as possible. I want her to be happy as much as you do," I say, trying anything to calm him down.

Lord, help me. Please! I scream over and over in my head.

"No one wants sissy happy like David does! Don't you try to take her from me! She's mine, I did this for her! So we could be a family again!" he screams, pressing the knife harder into her stomach. It tears her shirt and she drags in a ragged breath.

I wondered why she didn't try to speak, but now I see why. My necklace, the one I placed on her last night while she was sleeping, is choking her. David's headlock is yanking the chain taught, and my cross charm is digging into her throat, suffocating her, imprinting her with a symbol that should be a comforting object.

A tear slips down Katie's cheek and the silence seems to stretch on for minutes, but it's more like a few seconds. David takes a step backwards, dragging his sister by the neck. She loses her footing, sliding towards the ground, being held up completely by the arm of her brother. Katie starts thrashing, panicking, releasing strangled sobs as she tries to work free.

I charge. The sight of her lips turning blue and shirt growing bloodier by the second drives every ounce of fear from my body and I'm overcome with anger. Before I take three steps, another figure steps out of the shadows, her face red and jaw clenched as she smacks David on the back of the head with a baseball bat.

The impact is enough to force him to release Katie and she drops like a lead weight to the ground. Her brother is too stunned to react and his head whips back and forth between his sister on the ground and the brown haired girl holding a baseball bat. Sorren has never been strong, let alone strong enough to knock out a six-foot-four man.

Katie scrambles towards me on all fours and I rush to her, not embracing her, but shoving her behind me. I must push her harder than I thought, or she did it on purpose, because she falls to the ground with a grunt. I walk towards David, who is now brandishing a small revolver in his hand, the knife on the ground. He points the gun right at Sorren's chest, but his eyes remain locked on mine.

The change within them is horrifying. His gray-blue eyes go from raging mad to... blank. With pupils enlarged, face relaxed, and all emotion eliminated from his body, he laughs. The sound sends a shiver down my spine and I sprint the remaining feet between us, tackling him to the ground as the sound of a gunshot rings out.

Chapter 15

Katherine

I'm frozen in terror. The power behind my brother's hold is unlike anything I've ever felt before. Popping sounds fill my ears and the tears in my eyes are so thick I can't see anything. A chain from a necklace I don't remember wearing cuts into the skin around my neck, embedding itself into my flesh.

Tristan... I think, silently pleading with him to run. I know he won't, I wouldn't if our situations were reversed, but it's always worth a shot. I blink the tears from my eyes and they fall down my face before dripping onto David's sweaty arm.

My angel's eyes stare back at me, no longer feared with fear. Instead, an anger, in which I've never seen grace his eyes, fills him, contorting his face and making him stand taller. Tristan is a tall boy, but he has nothing on David's sheer size and muscle.

A blow comes from behind David and me, catching us both by surprise. He releases me and I catch my breath, my blood flowing again so quickly that I get dizzy. Tristan rushes towards me, but instead of holding me like I'd hoped he would, he pushes me behind him. The dizziness returns with a vengeance and I tumble to the ground, landing squarely on a large rock that cracks a few of my ribs. I hear the snaps, but don't feel the pain.

A gunshot rings out and I stop my labored breathing. Sorren lays sprawled on the ground a few feet from a tangled David and Tristan. Something hard hits me in the leg, and I pick it up. Another shot fills the air, making my ears ring, and the struggling boys on the ground continue fighting. I watch through blurry eyes as the sound of sirens breaks the loud silence. Red and blue lights cut through the mist that has formed over the land, and I lean against the truck, tucking my legs to my chest, as police officers rush towards us.

I put my face in my hands, shaking uncontrollably. The feel of cool metal presses against my cheek, and a dozen officers stand a few feet away from me, blocking Tristan and the scene that was just unfolding.

"Sweetheart, hand us the gun. You're safe now," a kind looking woman says, but with the gun she has pointed at me, I immediately see her as a threat.

The thing that hit my leg during the fight was the gun David had. Tristan must have gotten a hold of it and sent it flying wherever he could. I fired the second shot, the one that caused the ringing in my ears. I stare at the death trap in my hands before dropping it to the ground.

A man I don't recognize rushes over to me, momentarily letting me see what's unfolding beyond the circle of people I'm enclosed in. Tristan is sitting up, surrounded by his own group of officers. Sorren is being lifted onto a stretcher and from what I see, she isn't moving. A rock drops in my stomach, and I turn to the side and throw up on the shoes of the nearest officer. I look up at him to apologize, but more vomit makes an appearance.

The embarrassment from puking fades as I'm bombarded with pain from every orifice of my body. My torso feels like it's on fire, and trying to breathe sends stabbing pain to my lungs. I look at the ground, closing my mouth in an attempt to catch my breath. Every time I breathe in, I feel an agonizing pain in my ribs. The unknown man who was approaching me turns my face, but not before I catch sight of the blood on the ground. I didn't vomit; I was spewing blood.

"Katherine, we're going to take you to the hospital. This is oxygen, try to take slow breaths," the man says, trying to sound calm but his tone is laced with panic. He's young and probably inexperienced. Great... that's comforting.

The man loads me onto a gurney and plops me into the back of an ambulance, but not before Tristan hops in the back of the vehicle.

"Son, you can't be in here!" a man says, moving to push him out.

Tristan says nothing, merely sits beside me and takes my hand. He's in rough shape: a swollen eye that will probably be very black very soon, a deep gash on his forehead that looks like it needs stitches, and a split lip that coated his normally white teeth in a layer of crimson blood. The look in his eyes is all the reply the medic needs, because he shuts the door and we speed away.

Tears fall down Tristan's face and a sob escapes him; it's the first time I've ever seen him cry. I feel a heaviness settle over me, so I know I don't have long until I black out. I don't know what's wrong with me, or how serious my injuries are, so I don't want to waste another second by his side.

I raise my right hand, which is covered in blood and dirt, and sign Tristan the only word I know in sign language.

I love you.

Chapter 16

Tristan

I cry the whole way to the hospital. The medic didn't say a word as she passed out, just kept doing whatever he was doing to her. She told me she loves me. She didn't speak the words, but my sister and I used to sign them to each other every day as her school bus pulled away from our house. The gesture made more tears fall, and I was too heartbroken to care or be embarrassed.

The nurses had to pry my hand from Katie's as we entered the hospital, and I was left standing in the hallway, alone, with my angel's blood on my hands.

• •

Time passes. Who knows how much, but it passes. And I sit in the ER waiting room as doctors approach me. Questions. Stiches. Medication. It all blurs together until I take a deep breath...

And pray.

"Tristan?" I feel an arm pulling me upright and jump, eyes popping wide.

"Rachel," I say, accepting her hug with gratitude. She's been there for me through it all, so it only makes sense for her to be here with me now. Especially because it's her niece we're crying over this time.

"Thank you, Tristan. For being so brave," she says as I bury my face in her neck.

Brave? I'm blubbering like a child while she's consoling me. The only woman who has shown me maternal love in the past few years is the only person I speak to while we wait in the hospital. Doctors keep asking me to go get more thoroughly checked out, but I refuse.

"How's Sorren?" I ask as the latest round of nurses shuffles out of our private waiting room.

Rachel sighs, rubbing her temples with her fingers. It takes her a moment to answer, and it only takes a few seconds for me to get even more nervous.

"Sorren is in a coma, Tristan. She was shot in the head. They can't know the extent of the damage, and she's on life support," Rachel says.

My breath falls out of me in a huff. Emotional overload has officially set in and I slump against the bench and stop thinking.

Chapter 17

Katherine

The first thing I hear is someone talking. An unfamiliar female voice, which is rather nasally and unpleasant keeps repeating my name. My eyes open slowly and my lids feel like they weigh fifty pounds, but at least the room is semi-dark. They must've turned off the lights to help me adjust. It takes only a moment to remember my setting and when I do, a monitor registers the pickup of my heartbeat.

"Relax, Katherine. Do you know where you are? Don't try to speak, just nod if you do," she says with authentic concern in her eyes.

I nod and tears drip from my eyes. I hate crying, but it's all I seem to be doing of late.

"Good. Do you need any more pain medication? It will make you sleepy."

I shake my head, not wanting to sleep anymore. My whole body feels numb and I feel very vulnerable and being asleep would bring no comfort.

"Is it okay if we take out the tube that's down your throat?" she asks, completely serious.

I roll my eyes. *No, leave the tube in...* I think, loaded with sarcasm. The moment of irritation is erased as the tube is removed and I feel like I'm suffocating. I gasp and my lungs learn to work again.

"Great job, kiddo! I'll send the doctor in," the nurse says, patting my head like I'm a five year old. I resist the urge to roll my eyes again.

"Sorren. My friend. Is she okay?" I rasp, the words barely audible.

"I'll send the doctor in," the nurse repeats, worrying me.

A few seconds later, the same doctor I saw a few nights ago walks in. Doctor Colson.

"Katherine. Hello my dear. I'm sorry to see you again under these circumstances, but from what I hear, you're feeling well. You're not lying, I hope?" he says in his soothing deep voice.

Something about this man brings me comfort. I can't put my finger on it, but maybe he's just a genuinely nice person. I've always been a good judge of character. Minus the year...

"I'm not feeling *well*, but I'm not in as much pain as I thought I would be," I say, which is stupid. I wasn't thinking about the amount of pain I would be in. I've been thinking of nothing but Tristan and Sorren since I woke up a few minutes ago.

"How are my friends?" I ask, interrupting whatever he was beginning to say.

"Let's talk about you for a few minutes, Katherine," he insists, pulling over a little chair on wheels.

"Let's not. How are my friends?" I repeat with much more force.

He sighs, pulling off his overly large glasses. "Katherine, Sorena is in a coma. A bullet lodged in her brain and she's unable to function on her own. There isn't much we can do but pray."

The heart monitor slows down as a lead weight crashes onto my shoulders. I blink, but I am too stunned to show any emotion. My mind reels back to the visions we shared and the one I kept from her... of her death. Maybe they were warnings? But a coma isn't death. Miracles do exist, *I* am one of them. If it's meant to be, then it will be. It's the Lord's decision.

But that doesn't make it easy on the rest of us. A sudden realization falls on me and I scream before bursting into tears. It's still difficult to breathe, and I start gasping and panicking.

I was holding a gun. I fired a shot. What if it was my bullet that hit her? What if it was the bullet I released for no reason? I don't even remember why I shot! I just shot to feel like I was helping somehow. The doctor must have anticipated my meltdown because he puts a hand on my shoulder and speaks in a very firm voice.

"Katherine, Tristan saw the whole thing. David's bullet was what hit Sorren; not yours. You hit David in the shoulder, although no one knows how. You got extremely lucky, Miss. Prince. You have someone watching out for you up there," he concludes.

A few minutes pass and I try to even my breathing, like Doctor Colson instructs. He explains what happened to *me*, and I'm shocked to find that this whole ordeal took place nearly four days ago.

"You stumbled and landed, very hard and very fast, on a large, pointed rock. Upon impact, three of your ribs snapped and punctured your right lung. This is called pneumothorax, which is a collapsed lung. This condition is what caused you to cough up blood. We mended your lung but your ribs will have to heal on their own. We've kept you sedated so that you wouldn't be in pain," he says, sounding very professional.

I sniffle, wiping my nose with a tissue he hands me. "Is Tristan alright?" My heart thumps, waiting for an answer.

"Yes, other than a sprained wrist and a few cuts and bruises, he's miraculously unharmed. He hasn't left your side, or the waiting room, since your arrival. He's showering in the room next door at the moment. Your aunt is at the airport, picking up your mother."

A faint sigh of relief escapes me, followed quickly by guilt. How can I feel relieved when Sorren is in a coma? She took her life in her hands to protect us, the two people who fought with her the night before. The amount of courage it took, of love and selflessness, is astounding.

"Katie?" a voice says from the doorway.

My heart sings. The angel I've known for such a short time, but love so deeply, was almost taken from me. We were almost separated, and I had never told him how much he means to me. Never told him how thankful I am for his very soul; for his heart. He is all I've ever needed, desired, and dreamt of.

And he was almost gone as quickly as he came.

"Tristan," I say, voice cracking, but I refuse to cry. I also refuse to tell him my feelings in a hospital room, so close to death and heartbreak. So close to Sorren.

He closes the gap between us, gently wrapping his arms around me, being careful of my ribs. His one hand is wrapped in an Ace bandage, his forehead covered in gauze and eye black and blue. He looks like he took a jog through hell, but he is still beautiful. It's vain and horrible to notice such things under the circumstances, but I simply cannot help it.

His lips move but no words come out, and I know that he is praying. I close my eyes, feeling the blessings washing over me. The goodness flows out of every silent word he prays.

"Thank you, God," he says aloud, putting both hands on the sides of my head, kissing my forehead and letting his lips linger for a very long time.

Doctor Colson apparently stepped out of the room at some point, because when my eyes start to close and Tristan shuts off the lights completely, we are alone in my hospital room.

"You can go home tomorrow. We can get through this," Tristan whispers, dragging an uncomfortable looking chair over to my bedside.

"What happened to David?" I ask, almost not wanting to hear the answer.

"He's under arrest. He can't hurt anyone anymore."

A few moments pass by. "Tristan?" I whisper, unsure if he fell asleep.

"Yes, angel?"

I hesitate. "Don't sleep in the chair, please. I just... just want to feel you holding me," I squeak out, choking back tears yet again.

He doesn't object, just moves the railing down on the left side of my bed and takes off his shoes. I scoot over until my hip bumps the right railing, but there is a surprising amount of room for a hospital bed. Tristan climbs in next to me, sharing my pillow and gently wrapping an arm around my stomach, using his other arm as extra support under his head. I turn on my side, which isn't an easy task due to the shooting pain in my chest. Tristan must sense this because he shifts, leaning over my body and pressing the red button on the bed.

"Yes, Katherine?"

"She needs some more pain medicine, please," Tristan says, speaking for me.

Not a minute later the nurse comes in, using the light from the open door to inject medication into my IV and, almost immediately, drowsiness settles over me. The nurse doesn't say anything about our intimate position; just bids us a goodnight and shuts the door behind her.

Our legs intertwine, our breaths mix, and I fall asleep with his lips on mine.

■■

I'm woken the next morning by sunlight hitting me directly in the face. Tristan is still curled up next to me, looking very uncomfortable. In two chairs next to my bed, not speaking to one another, are my Aunt Rachel and my mother. I blink a few times, feeling stiffness in my neck and back. The pain in my chest is still present every time I inhale, but I can't not breathe so I better get used to it because, according to Doctor Colson, ribs take at least six weeks to heal.

"Katherine?" my mother says, keeping her voice low.

I look over at her and our eyes connect, a secret and silent message being sent between us. Something in her eyes says more than any sentence we've ever shared before. The inner conflict raging within her green eyes, so like my own, speaks volumes: she's sorry, she loves me, and she wishes she could take everything back. Every time she stood by as my father broke a piece of my heart with his words or his fists. Every time she should've comforted me when instead she ignored the truth.

If I wasn't God's child, if I rejected his love and is word, then I would not have the strength to do what I am about to do. I would simply walk away and let the bitterness consume me. But instead, I take God's love and use it to the fullest.

"Hi Mom," I say, but my voice crackles from disuse.

She must see the forgiveness in my eyes, because she starts to cry. I've never actually seen my mother cry in person, only in the vision I had of my suicide. It's disarming to see her vulnerable, but it's about time.

"We'll go get the doctor, Katherine. It's time you get out of here, huh?" Aunt Rachel says as she stands and plants a kiss on my forehead. I smile up at her through the drowsiness and she exits the room with my mother on her heels.

I put my hand on Tristan's face, inches from my own. Almost immediately he stirs, groaning as the light from the window hurts his tired eyes. He moves his arm and his shoulder pops, showing me how poorly he must have slept last night.

"Good morning," I say as he rubs his face with his hands. There's a bit of stubble on his chin, which adds to the rugged look of his face. How does someone so beautiful, even in the early morning with bruises all over his face and bags under his eyes, belong to me? I don't know, but I'm sure glad he does.

The doctor comes in with nurses and in the next hour, I'm being rolled to the car in a wheelchair. It's cramped in the backseat with Tristan next to me and my mother in the front, but we manage to get home in one piece.

The sun makes its way across the sky, signifying the passage of time. Tristan and I sit on the porch, staring at the mountains, not speaking. I don't think there are words right now, so we comfort each other in silence.

My brother is responsible for the deaths of multiple people, and for the nearly fatal injury of the girl I share some sort of connection with. The girl who risked her life to save mine and my angel's. My brother, the boy I took baths with, lived with, slept a room away from, *cowered* with as our father beat our mother in front of our eyes, is capable of *murder*.

I am ashamed to be of his homicidal blood. I am angry that he took the lives of so many people for no reason. I am confused as to what made him snap and decide that the lives of others were worthless. Trying to get inside the mind of a killer is useless, so I must stop attempting to understand. Because the truth is, we'll never know. The sibling I thought I loved and missed and understood is no more. Perhaps he never was; he was merely a figment of my wishful thinking. Perhaps he was always lethal and he finally decided that he was tired of hiding his need for blood.

Of course he would go after our father. I should be mourning his death, like any good daughter would do. But he was not a good father, so I don't owe him a single tear. As God's child, I'm trying to find it in my heart to forgive his soul for the abuse he inflicted on his family for so many years. The abuse that led to my self-loathing and, ultimately, attempted suicide.

No, I do not mourn the death of the man who drove me to such pain. Who broke my heart into a hundred tiny pieces, some lost forever in dark pits, never to be found again. I mourn for a life lost at the hands of a psychopath, but I would be lying if I said he didn't deserve it. No one deserves to die, but this is his own form of punishment. I had intensified emotions, but he gets an eternity to reflect on his atrocities.

I wonder what my mother is feeling. What went through her mind as she watched her son lose whatever was left of his sanity? What does she think of the miraculous recovery her suicidal delinquent daughter made? Does she blame herself for David's acts? Wonder how I was healed and her son wasn't?

The love of God saved my soul and brought me out of the darkness that almost swallowed me. His love, his pure unbiased *love* filled my heart with a brightness that no amount of therapy or medication or alcohol could ever compete with. The peace inside of me is only there because he believed in me enough to give me life after I took it away.

I feel a sudden urge to take a hike, but my body is in no shape to walk all the way to our spot.

"Tristan?" I say, shattering the silence that formed a bubble around me.

"Yeah?"

"Does my aunt still have that ATV?" I ask, remembering her talking about the machine many years ago.

Apparently she does, because not ten minutes later I find myself seated on it in front of Tristan, who surprisingly didn't object to taking a ride. *Maybe he feels the same need I do*, I wonder to myself.

The ride is slow and bump free, not jostling my broken ribs any more than absolutely necessary. The pain is bearable with the amount of medication in my system, and when we arrive at our cliff, with the lake reflecting the sunlight like a mirror, I feel an instant calmness.

This is where Tristan and I learned to share. This is where I learned to love. It's only appropriate that this is the place I make the most important declaration of my life.

We sit, him carefully helping me place my feet over the edge of the rock structure. The sun blinds me momentarily, but my eyes soon adjust to the light. The landscape is still stunning, taking what little breath I have away for a second. It's a crystal clear day, not a cloud in the sky. The storm from a few nights ago is nothing but a distant memory as I listen to the leaves rustling, a sweet and loving breeze causing the trees to wave at us.

"Thank you, Tristan. Thank you for saving me. For protecting me," I say, voice showing no sign of cracking or breaking; completely and totally firm.

He puts his head in his hands, not replying. After a few minutes, I grow anxious.

"What's the matter?" I ask, which is a stupid question because there are a number of answers.

"I pushed you, Katie. You fell and almost *died* because of me! I'm so sorry," he says, sounding anguished.

I'm shocked. Misplaced guilt is tearing away at him; I can see it in his beautiful blue eyes. My heart aches at the sight of him so distressed, and I wonder if this is why he's been so quiet and remote.

"Tristan, you saved my life. I tripped on my own two feet because I was dizzy, you didn't push me. Don't you dare blame yourself for this," I warn, pointing one finger at him.

He says nothing, just stares at me, his eyes roaming over my face. Whatever he finds there must be enough to satisfy him and relieve a bit of the guilt imprinted into his baby blues. His hand reaches up to cup my cheek and his thumb caresses my lower lip. I smile a little, unable to help it.

I lean over and kiss him, *really* kiss him, for the second time since our first kiss only a few days ago. He flinches and I pull back, forgetting about his injured lip. I open my mouth to apologize, but he closes his lips over mine before I can speak.

This kiss is much sweeter than anything before it. He touches me softly, careful not to disturb any random injuries on my body. Soon enough, I end up lying on top of him, the sun beating on my back, warming my skin through my shirt. The pressure on my ribs hurts, but I don't care. His hands roam and so do mine as the thought of losing him shoots through my mind again, causing me to push myself closer to him, wanting to consume him.

The kiss goes from innocent to heated as the minutes pass, something I haven't experienced in quite some time. I can feel his emotion pouring out of him, but only through his actions. There is absolutely no reminder of my punishment at all, except for the dull memories. It seems like a distant dream, my life before God. My life before Tristan. Before salvation.

A bird swoops dangerously low to our tangled bodies, and I break our kiss out of shock. He grips the back of my head and I think he's about to pull me back in, so I just spit out what I brought him here to say.

"I love you," I say, but it melts together with his words, the exact ones that just came from my heart to his ears. He loves me. *He loves me.*

I gasp as my vision suddenly cuts off, sending me spiraling down a black tunnel into nothingness.

Chapter 18

My eyes spring open and I find myself sitting on a park bench, dressed in my favorite sundress. Water laps at the rocks by the shore in front of me, and I recognize the beach from my dream; the dream where Tristan told me he loves me.

I blink, and when my eyes open, Tristan is sitting beside me. We look at one another, utterly confused but unafraid. A magnificent, familiar feeling washes over us simultaneously. My head turns without my permission towards the man standing in front of us, dressed in a turquoise robe with blonde hair and bare feet. I bow my head, instantly aware of whom the man is.

The man is God.

"Children," he says, his voice sweeter than any sound I've ever heard. It's as if every symphony ever played, every song ever written and every lyric in the universe joined together to create a most precious sound that usually falls deaf on human ears.

"Father," Tristan and I say in unison, reveling in the warmth coming off the man who gave us a second chance at life.

"I know you're confused, but I thank you for your faith and trust in knowing that I will help you understand," the Lord says, grabbing my left hand and Tristan's right. "Come, let us walk," he says, so we walk.

The water doesn't seem so beautiful now; it pales in comparison to the man walking between us. My entire body feels better than it ever has before, like there are no broken ribs or broken pieces of my heart. I feel utterly and completely happy.

"You have shared many lives together, children. It is against my wishes to reincarnate souls, but you are two of four exceptions. I think you know who the other two are, correct?"

I nod, knowing that he is referring to David and Sorren. The only two people in my vision that I know.

"Yes, Katherine. Sorena and David. You see, centuries ago I created your souls, fashioning you in my image and connecting you in a way only true soul mates are connected. You were meant to be all each other needed, a perfect set," he says, leisurely walking us down a strip of deserted path.

"Every human being in the universe has at least one of these soul mates, a person who helps you become what I created you to become. They find each other before their physical life ends, and their purpose is made possible if they only tried. If they only opened their hearts to my kingdom, they would fulfill all their potential and more. You see, I am the creator of Fate; we work together and mold the future of the souls that will walk the Earth. With the help of the angels, we keep the humans happy and fulfilled.

"But, as you know, the world is no longer a place of perfection, as it was intended to be. I was betrayed, and Satan became my enemy. He works with his legion of follows to enter the realm where Fate weaves the future of my children. There, he wreaks havoc on the souls too weak to resist. It isn't often Fate makes a mistake, but Satan is a snake and always finds ways to slither into even the smallest of holes."

I feel the understanding wash over me, filling the gaps in my mind like a solved mystery. The Lord continues speaking and we keep walking, listening ardently.

"Human souls have a divine connection to the Realm of Fate, and when Satan enters the realm and your soul has the slightest weak moment, your earthly body is under attack. Your first lives, children, were during the time of the vision you had, Katherine. Your world was turned upside down. Tristan was framed for a child's murder by a rogue mafia assassin.

"You and Tristan were married, Katherine. You were expecting your first child, to be a girl named Skylar, a very unique name for the era. It is not in her destiny to live a long life, because her soul is too fragile. Satan entered your Fate, children. He cursed your love with a swipe of his sword and your souls were unprepared for the attack. You have lived two lives since the original slashing of your Fates, and only now have your souls mended. You believe in me, have turned your life to my love, and that change has restored your souls to their state.

"Sorena and David for that matter have refused to join my kingdom again. David's Fate has been lost to Satan, never again to reborn or remade. Sorena, first born Cassandra Clintock in the year 1850, is suspended in the Realm of Fate, her soul unable to make a decision. She believes enough in me to be reborn again, but only if she chooses to. Modern medicine describes her state as a coma, which I have disguised her conflict as. In actuality, her soul is trying to fight its way out of Satan's grasp, which she has clung to so strongly in the past.

"Sorena has a kind enough soul to win the battle, but it will not be an easy task. She will have to be reborn in order to set the universe right again. You see, children, every soul has a purpose and every life lived is intertwined, adding to the future of the universe as a whole. When Satan skews Fate, the universe is thrown off kilter. This is why we have murders. This is why there are starving children and drugs and pain. Satan takes my plans and uses them against me."

The last pieces of my broken heart click together as the mysteries that have been haunting me are solved. There are no accurate words for how I feel at this moment, but I can only hope Tristan feels this way too.

"Lastly, this will be the last you see of me until your human lives are over. I love you, my children," God says, swinging around to face us head on. "I bless you for your faith and courage, and I am proud to be your Father. My kingdom will always be open to you, and may you rest well knowing you will enter it after this life. May you grow old together, enjoy your children and do what you are destined to accomplish. The universe is righted a little more with the healing of your hearts, and may you always know that Satan cannot touch you."

I reach out my arms, wanting to hold the man responsible for saving me. He opens his, embracing me, filling me with light and love. Tristan does the same and we huddle together, Father and his children united once more.

"Oh, let me say one more thing. Your human minds will not remember a moment of this, or any of our meetings. Memories of your visions will be erased, all reminders of your Punishments eliminated, and your knowledge of what I just told you will not be accessible as long as you are on Earth. In your hearts, you will be content and know that I am taking care of you, but your minds will be wiped clean of any and all burdens that may have accompanied these divine visits.

"Live well, my children. You will do wonderful things. Go in peace and know that I am God, and I am waiting for you," he says, kissing each of our foreheads before walking down the path, still facing us, never turning his back.

Tristan and I grasp hands, watching the Lord raise a staff before everything goes black.

Chapter 19

I awake from possibly the most restful nap I've ever had in my life. My body is sprawled across Tristan's, lined up from chest to toes. I giggle, wondering how we ever fell asleep like this.

"Wake up, Tristan," I coo, but that doesn't work so I kiss him awake. His eyes spring open and the lovely light azure color brings a smile to my face.

"Hey, beautiful. I don't remember falling asleep," he says, rubbing his eyes with his hands.

"Me either. But I don't really want to move right now, so can we just stay here for a while?" I say, wrapping my arms tighter around his neck. The motion ignites a very slight soreness in my torso and it takes me a moment to remember my injuries. They aren't even half as painful as Doctor Colson warned me they would be, and Tristan's face is already healed, after only five days.

He chuckles, the sound vibrating in his chest onto my cheek, which is pressed against his heart. "I can't remember when we fell asleep. What were we talking about?"

I struggle for a moment to regain my memory, but then the last words we spoke flash through my mind and I feel guilty for not remembering them immediately.

"You told me that you love me," I say, pushing his hair back from his forehead, smiling. "And I told you that I love you."

He smiles as he answers, "That's what I thought. I just wanted to hear you say it again."

I laugh and mock slap him, gently tapping his heavenly face with my palm. He traps it in his hand and whips me onto my back, suddenly but still gently enough not to hurt me on the rock beneath us. His lips find mine and his hands move over every line of my body as he kisses me beneath the sun, which shines brighter than I've ever seen before, lighting my world with its warm rays.

I feel unlike I ever have before: capable of anything and totally free. My burdens over David's attack are nonexistent and I'm not sure why, but something tells me not to dwell on facts. Call it divine intervention, a sixth-sense, whatever you want... but all I know is that I'm right where I'm supposed to be.

．．．

Chapter 21

The rest of the year at Shields Valley High School went by without a hitch: I made honor roll, made lots of friends and completely remade my reputation. Tristan joined the lacrosse team in the spring, earning him a scholarship to Northwestern University and back into the good graces of the entire community.

David was charged with six counts of murder and three attempted murders, and a death sentence was served, bringing peace of mind to everyone in the saddest possible way. It's heartbreaking to see a life so consumed by evil that they must be put to death, but it's for the best I assume. I no longer refer to David as "my brother," and his sentence was far easier to bear than I would have ever thought.

Yes, our small town was shocked for a few weeks, unsure of what to do with all the media attention. My classmates were shaken by the fact that one of their own peers was the sister of a now notorious killer, but the whispers and concerned looks stopped after a few months. My mother moved back to Chicago, but she and I maintain weekly contact, mending our relationship one step at a time. She dealt with the death of my father fairly well, knowing he couldn't hurt her or their daughter anymore. I am frequently saddened by the way his life turned out, but something tells me I have no reason to mourn.

Sorren is still in a coma, living with the assistance of a machine, unable to survive on her own. Doctors have told us that coma patients have been some of the most miraculous recoveries in the medicine world, but I know it's up to her. Sorren is strong enough to pull through, so I'll always be waiting for my friend. I will never forget her and I think of her every day. She's in every prayer I whisper and every hymn I sing, but there is a peace in my heart for no reason, forbidding me to be depressed over her situation.

"Ready?" a voice says from behind me, muscular arms wrapping around me.

I sigh, placing my hands over his. "Yes," I say, stretching my neck up to kiss his chin, hovering just above my shoulder.

"Then let's go, angel," Tristan says, pulling me towards the door of his apartment, where I stayed last night, only after reassuring my aunt that Tristan would sleep on the couch. Being trusted feels wonderful. Being legally eighteen feels even better.

"Why did you ever start calling me that?" I ask as we hop in his truck, carefully tucking our robes inside the doors.

He chuckles, grabbing my hand as we pull onto the street. "I have no idea, but you're so perfect, I can only assume you're heaven sent," he jokes, winking, which makes me laugh and mock-punch him in the side.

We pull up to the school that has been my home for the past eight months and sit in the truck, reflecting on what was probably the craziest year of our lives. We both miraculously survived attempted suicides, but I can't even remember what possessed me to try to kill myself. That was a time in my life that apparently dragged me so far under water that I blocked it out completely. Aunt Rachel tells me that things like "mental block" happen a lot to trauma patients, but here's my theory: God gave me a chance to start anew, making my bad memories hazy and giving me a completely new slate. What makes me special enough to deserve that, I have no idea. But thanks to my faith, I have a constant feeling that everything is going to be alright.

Times speeds up and before I know it, we're standing on the stage. Tristan is standing in front of me, as we are lined up alphabetically, and he is next to be called by Vice Principal Nicholson.

Miss. Nicholson speaks, her voice blasting through the speakers for the whole town to hear. "Tristan Presidio, graduate with honors, member of the National Honors Society, and recipient of the Presidential Alumni Scholarship to Northwestern University in Illinois where he will be studying engineering."

The clapping in the room is thunderous, the town celebrating the walking miracle that is Tristan Presidio. Tears fill my eyes and a wave of thoughts flood my head. What if we had never met? Fate is what brought us together, I'm sure of it. If I had never met Tristan, my faith wouldn't be as strong as it is now. My faith wouldn't have had the power to bring me out of the darkness that seemed so constant.

I wouldn't be the person I am now if it weren't for the hardships in my life. I have survived abuse, suicide, emotional torment and a hostage situation, all in a span of eighteen years. I have been kicked, bruised, broken, and had my heart shattered into a million pieces by the people that should have meant the most to me.

I was weak, but now I am strong. I was alone, now I have a family. I was empty, but now I am filled. It took death, destruction and heartache to get me to where I am, but I am proud of the person I have become.

"Katherine Prince, graduate with advanced honors, member of the National Honors Society, and recipient of the Susan Caputi Scholarship to Northwestern University in Illinois, where she will be studying psychology," says Miss. Nicholson.

The steps towards my principal seem to take a lifetime, but once I'm there, I feel as if everything is happening at warped-speed. Clapping fills the auditorium and I spot my mother and Aunt Rachel snapping pictures in the third row. I descend the stairs and impatiently wait until they finish calling students.

"Congratulations to the class of 2014. Live well, pupils. I have no doubt you will do wonderful things," our principal announces, and the sentiment feels achingly familiar.

I don't have time to ponder my curiosity, because caps are flying towards the ceiling and arms are wrapping around me. Person after person embraces me, passing me through the crowd like a ragdoll. I trip on a stray foot and tumble into the arms of the person I love more than anything in this world.

"Congratulations, angel. Looks like we made it after all," he says, holding me close. "Thank you, for being all I need and all I want."

Tears form in my eyes and spill over, but not out of sadness. Joy is what causes the wetness in my eyes to drip down my face, and Tristan wipes my tears away with his thumbs, but more fall. I am overjoyed with the knowledge that this is a new beginning, a chance to help others and do something that will leave an impact on the world.

"Let's get out of here, shall we?" Tristan asks, looking like he needs to escape the crowd.

I nod and we basically sprint towards his truck, tears still falling and leaking into my mouth through my smile.

"Where do you want to go?"

The statement is very literal in this moment, but it registers with much more depth. I can go anywhere I want to from here, because this is my life now. I have all I need and want sitting next to me and the light that is our future is so bright it blinds me for a moment.

"Anywhere."

● ●

Epilogue

"Ready?" a voice asks from behind me as arms encircle me in their warmth. I sink into their embrace for only a moment before whipping around, returning to my hasty state of undress.

"Do I *look* ready, Tristan? I can't believe you sprung this on me!" I say, walking over to our closet and pulling out a black cocktail dress. I slide my towel to the floor and wiggle into the most perfect dress I have ever owned.

Tristan leans against the doorframe, watching me with an amused expression. "Angel, it's just me. You don't need makeup to be beautiful," he says, just trying to placate me. It works.

I put on my red high heels, which add at least four inches to my legs, bringing me closer to Tristan's six-foot-two height.

"You, sir, are lucky you're so damn adorable. Otherwise I would be beyond pissed at you right now for springing a fancy dinner on me with an hour notice!" I say, jabbing him in the chest with my finger, but he just grabs my hand and pulls me towards the door.

We're sitting at our favorite fancy restaurant, the one we go to at least once a month, for no real reason other than we like to enjoy ourselves. Our apartment is right down the block, so we walk instead of driving.

"What do you think about me getting my last name changed to my mother's maiden name?" I ask as I sip my coke.

Tristan doesn't look surprised. We've talked about this before. "If you're hell-bent on changing your last name..." he shakes his head, sounding irritated.

He's told me numerous times that he loves my last name and that I shouldn't let the past define my future, but I can't have a successful career as a psychiatrist when all everyone thinks of when they hear my name is *David Prince, psycho killer.*

"If you're hell-bent on changing your last name," he repeats, recapturing my attention. He knows exactly when I space out. Tristan stands, making me raise my eyebrows in confusion. "Then why don't you change it to mine?"

He kneels in front of me, pulling a box out of his jacket pocket and opening it. The ring inside is perfect, just like the man holding it. My world is finally complete, the grievances of the past forgotten.

As he slides the ring on my finger, the last piece of my mending heart clicks into place. At last, I am finally whole.

The End

Acknowledgements

First and foremost I want to thank the Lord for giving me the inspiration and willpower to write a novel about his everlasting love... and for giving me my very own second chance.

My entire family for encouraging me and keeping my spirits high when all I wanted to do was rip my hair out. Mom, Aunt Dee, Aunt Lori, and Nani, thanks for being the four most amazing women in my life, and I love you all very much.

Laura, Jennifer, Catie, Sammy, Hailey Rose, Julia and Alexis for showing me that God really is in those around us. Thanks to all my other friends and teachers at Mount St. Mary's for urging me to keep writing Katherine and Tristan's story.

Lastly, thank you to Mrs. Schiavone, Mr. Rajczak, and Mr. Feltges for instilling in me a love of writing and literature I didn't know existed in my heart. To you I will always be grateful, because it was the three of you who helped me see the beauty in the words around me. I will never forget the lessons I've learned from you, so thank you. Thank you. Thank you.

About the Author

Kristina Rovison is a high school junior, born and raised in Buffalo, New York. She has a passion for literature and writing stories with the hopes of inspiring others. If you wish to contact her, look for her author page on Facebook, www.facebook.com/KristinaMRovisonYAauthor.

Be on the lookout for Kristina's second novel, releasing in the summer of 2013.

Made in the USA
Charleston, SC
20 September 2012